T0166740

A VIEW OF STARS

Stories of Love

EDITED BY
ANITHA DEVI PILLAI &
FELIX CHEONG

Marshall Cavendish
Editions

© 2021 Marshall Cavendish International (Asia) Private Limited

Published by Marshall Cavendish Editions
An imprint of Marshall Cavendish International

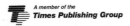

A member of the
Times Publishing Group

All rights reserved

No part of this publication may be reproduced, stored in a retrieval system or transmitted, in any form or by any means, electronic, mechanical, photocopying, recording or otherwise, without the prior permission of the copyright owner. Requests for permission should be addressed to the Publisher, Marshall Cavendish International (Asia) Private Limited, 1 New Industrial Road, Singapore 536196. Tel: (65) 6213 9300. E-mail: genref@sg.marshallcavendish.com
Website: www.marshallcavendish.com

The publisher makes no representation or warranties with respect to the contents of this book, and specifically disclaims any implied warranties or merchantability or fitness for any particular purpose, and shall in no event be liable for any loss of profit or any other commercial damage, including but not limited to special, incidental, consequential, or other damages.

Other Marshall Cavendish Offices:
Marshall Cavendish Corporation, 800 Westchester Ave, Suite N-641, Rye Brook, NY 10573, USA • Marshall Cavendish International (Thailand) Co Ltd, 253 Asoke, 16th Floor, Sukhumvit 21 Road, Klongtoey Nua, Wattana, Bangkok 10110, Thailand • Marshall Cavendish (Malaysia) Sdn Bhd, Times Subang, Lot 46, Subang Hi-Tech Industrial Park, Batu Tiga, 40000 Shah Alam, Selangor Darul Ehsan, Malaysia

Marshall Cavendish is a registered trademark of Times Publishing Limited

National Library Board, Singapore Cataloguing in Publication Data
Name(s): Pillai, Anitha Devi, editor. | Cheong, Felix, editor.
Title: A view of stars : stories of love / edited by Anitha Devi Pillai & Felix Cheong.
Description: Singapore : Marshall Cavendish Editions, [2020]
Identifier(s): OCN 1198974906 | ISBN 978-981-49-2807-6 (paperback)
Subject(s): LCSH: Love--Fiction. | Short stories.
Classification: DDC S823--dc23

Printed in Singapore

Poem "I Watch the Stars Go Out" by Felix Cheong from
I Watch the Stars Go Out (Ethos Books, 1999).

Cover image: Shutterstock

For Theijes Therrat Menon,
may you find a love that brings you
a lifetime of unbridled joy and comfort.
– ADP

For Dad and Mom,
in remembrance and love.
– FC

CONTENTS

PREFACE

★ ★ ★

What love is, when love is not. How love is, why love is not.

We can peel its petals many times over but the sunflower that is love remains as bright and unyielding, its face always opening to the light.

It is a thing of splendour and beauty: child-likeness and sometimes, the likeness of a child; aged and at times, damaged; hellbent and oftentimes, a godsend.

We can sing of its mysteries and hurts, its giving and forgiving ways, how it bends and mends.

In praise or lament of love, we have written arias and pop songs, plays and parables, movies and TV shows, books and poems, Facebook posts and blogs. Indeed, generations have generated words that wound around wounds, and band-aid of pages that began in remembrances past and looking to infinity ahead.

Yet, in spite it all – or because of it – love is its own cliché. All we can say about it, hand to heart, a kiss hovering in the air, is it still moves, like God, in mysterious ways. We experience and know it, in our time, by our own reckoning. And by its particularity and peculiarity, love is paradoxically universal.

It was the universal traits of love that was the topic of conversation one morning between Anitha Devi Pillai and Anita Teo that planted the seed for this anthology. Both had love stories of their strong-willed grandmothers to share and when Felix Cheong joined the conversation, he too had one about his parents. The conversation continued with other writers and seventeen heart-warming and memorable stories were collected, many of which were inspired by true events or by well-known epic tales. The stories include author commentaries that provide an additional lens to understand the writers' inspiration and creation.

This book would not have been possible without the unwavering faith of managing editor Anita Teo, senior editor Shereen Wong and designer Lynn Chin. We are deeply grateful that they helped to weave their magic in making this book a reality. We are also indebted to Assistant Professor Wernmei Yong Ade for her kind endorsement of this anthology as well as the fifteen authors who have contributed stories to this book.

We hope that *A View of Stars: Stories of Love* will make your heart smile and sigh with us.

Anitha Devi Pillai
Felix Cheong

I WATCH THE STARS GO OUT

Felix Cheong

Perhaps love
is a view of stars
through the telescope of years,
now aged,
no longer uncommitted
in chosen places
nor fearful
of that strident moment
when light explodes
into a million shards of heart.

BYGONE

YEARS

★ ★ ★

AN UNUSUAL ARRANGEMENT

Anitha Devi Pillai

★ ★ ★

It was a new day in 1924 and a special birthday for Chellamma; for not only had she turned twelve, her wedding too was barely a few hours away.

Her mother had woken her up at dawn to give her an extra-long massage that day with homemade oil made from coconut, red hibiscus flowers and almonds from their garden. Each family in the village had their own concoction of oil but theirs was the most coveted one. The villagers believed that Chellamma's family's pitch-black hair and youthful skin were attributed to their weekly oil baths and massages using their family's century-old secret blend of homemade oil. No one in her family had grey hair nor wrinkled skin – well, at least not until one was in their late seventies.

To her great annoyance, she was not allowed to swim and linger in their family's fresh-water pond with her cousins, despite it being a special day. Instead, all she had for company that morning was her grandmother and aunts.

"Bathe quickly! What will they say about our family if you are not dressed when they arrive? And don't go climbing trees for mangos with Gopalan … did you hear me?"

Chellamma rolled her eyes in annoyance. She had not even seen Gopalan in the last two days.

Everyone had something to say to her that morning. After more rituals and prayers, she was ushered into a room on the upper floor of their two-storey house. Now that she was to be married in a few hours, she was told that this was her room henceforth. It was her favourite room in the house as it faced their village's only river. The womenfolk had more instructions on her new daily routine from the next day onwards as a married woman. She barely paid attention to what the women were saying.

"I wonder if he is handsome."

She had not meant to speak those words aloud. But the women in the room understood her. None of them had seen the groom either. All they knew was that she was lucky to marry him as he was a man of considerable means and grit. He had, after all, left the comforts of his sprawling home at the age of sixteen in search of a job in Singapore. Rumour had it that he was not on the best of terms with his maternal uncle and was eager to fly the coop as soon as he could. And now having made his own fortune, he had returned, at the age of twenty-one. This time he was ready to 'take a bride' in his hometown.

Soon it was time and her grandmother entered her room with her family jewellery, a stunning two-piece cotton sari with thick gold borders and a blouse that stopped a few inches below her breasts. Chellamma was the first amongst them to don a blouse under the sari wrapped around her chest for her wedding. In keeping with the times, she did not have a hair wound into a round coil on the side of her head. Instead, her mother parted Chellamma's luxurious thick hair in the centre and plaited it loosely. The womenfolk, who were gathered in the hallway, cooed in delight when they saw her for the first time in her wedding attire, remarking how times had changed in their ancestral home.

The day itself was etched in her memory, for that was when she met him – her Krishnan.

She had been impatient to get a glimpse of him without being seen from the western wing of the house where the women stood. She tiptoed and craned her neck over her aunts' shoulders just as he entered her home with an entourage largely made up of bare-chested men in stark white dhotis and a piece of white cloth over their shoulders.

Krishnan was a tall man with broad shoulders and at least two heads taller than all the men in her family. He certainly looked so out of place in her home in his long-sleeved white cotton shirt that he had rolled up just above his elbows and khaki-coloured pants from Singapore. He was also the first man that she had seen in her community who did not spot a tuft of hair on his head.

But he didn't notice her. Like everyone else in the room, he too was transfixed by the hanging brass oil lamps around the four sides of the courtyard and the sight of the 1,001 lotus flowers her older brother Gopalan had gathered to decorate the courtyard. Delicately strung lotus garlands were woven around the teakwood pillars and brass chains holding up the oil lamps. There were purplish-pink lotus flowers in every nook and cranny. It was unusual to decorate the home so extravagantly for a wedding ceremony. In years to come, the village folk would reminisce about a brother foraging the surrounding villages for his sister's favourite flowers to decorate the palatial house up the hill.

For all the hurry-burry that had consumed their home earlier in the day, the ceremony itself was a simple one. Krishnan was made to sit on a wooden plank next to a brightly lit tall oil lamp in the middle of their courtyard. Chellamma was instructed to kneel on the ground in front of him by her oldest aunt. As custom dictated, she faced east. She faced him.

"She looks tiny!" said someone seated on the left. Relatives were gathered around the four sheltered sides of the open courtyard.

Under the shimmering light from the stars of the midnight blue sky above, Krishnan carefully placed a traditional Kerala sari much like what she was wearing in her hands.

"Hello ... I'm Balakrishnan," he said in English. A few of her relatives sniggered. Someone said something naughty leading to more giggles from her cousins standing on the far left of the courtyard.

He wasn't supposed to speak to her until they were alone. But he was hardly like any of the other men in the room. He was the "foreign-returned groom" and as such, forgiven for his transgressions.

She didn't pay any heed to the whispers around her. Gossip and small talk never bothered her. All she could think of at that moment was that, for a man built like a wrestler, Krishnan had a gentle voice.

She spied bottles of gingelly oil for her hair, foreign-looking perfume bottles, areca nuts and betel leaves on the gift trays that his relatives had brought for her. Her aunt then sprinkled rice over both their heads and shoulders. With that, the wedding ceremony ended. But the fragrance of the lotus flowers lingered in the air for several days, reminding her of new status.

The next few years were blissful and they were blessed with three children. But for a man who had tasted independence at a young age, he was restless and homesick for the sounds and smells of Singapore.

He regaled her with stories of roads so wide and clean you could sleep on them and about the people of different races whom he had worked with. He taught her several Malay words that he had picked up. Everyone in Singapore spoke Malay most of the time and English sometimes, he said. He told her that people were the same underneath and that they had more in common than they knew. That both Chinese and Malayalees believed that the gates of the underworld were thrown open at the same time of the year. While Malayalees celebrated the occasion with a feast and lighting oil lamps to welcome their King Mahabali from the underworld and called it Onam, the Chinese welcomed their ancestors by laying out a feast for them on the streets and burning joss sticks for their blessings. They called it the Hungry Ghost Festival.

"*Aiyee* …. So, all the underworld subjects take a holiday in Malaya? Even, they take a holiday … and travel long distance!"

They burst out laughing in the dead of the night, annoying the family dog who started howling. That only made them laugh harder.

"Are there any Malayalee women there? What do the *Singapur* women look like? Who is prettier? I or the women in small frocks in *Singapur*?"

He sidestepped some of her questions. He knew she was just teasing him.

"The women are so beautiful … you should meet my boss, Devanathan Pillay's wife … she is …"

"They are Malayalees?"

"Noooo ... my boss is a Chetti Melaka. They are half-Malay and half-Indian ... who knows ... maybe they do have Malayalee roots."

"Ahh ... okay ... Did you have a girlfriend in *Singapur*?" she asked in jest, another day, not really expecting him to answer.

"Well ... for a while, I thought Pillay's wife liked me. She was quite young ... younger than me. One day, when I went to collect Pillay's lunch, she asked me if I could get her a traditional Kerala sari. She spoke for a long time about how good-looking our people were. She touched my arm once or twice. I was only nineteen years old ... I thought ... oh ... you know ... well, you know what giving a woman a sari means in our culture ... I thought that was a hint."

Chellamma attempted to smother the laughter that rose up from her belly in his chest. But her heaving laughter got him laughing too, albeit rather sheepishly. In retrospect, it was funny. He had been heartbroken for a while when he realised that all she wanted was to cut up the sari that he had gifted her to make into a skirt. He had gone to great lengths to procure a new Kerala sari from a friend's family.

"*Aiyoh*! These foreigners ... you know ... my Malayalam Miss (Malayalam teacher) told my class a story once about a Governor of Madras, a British man, a Sir Mou ... something something Duff, who offered a lady in Travancore ... maybe was it our Travancore Queen ... I don't know ... well apparently he offered her a beautiful fabric from Madras right in front of her family ..."

Neither of them could stop giggling as it was clear where the story was headed.

"She goes ... no ... no ... thank you, sir ... I am quite satisfied with my present husband ... I can't accept your fabric ..."

They squealed in laughter and almost rolled off their bed.

She had a million other questions for him every night. And he was only too eager to quell her curiosity with tales that often sounded too good to be true of a land far away, filled with strange practices and ways.

"You know, Chellam, they are not like us ... there is a stigma about divorce. Women don't leave their husbands. All of them ... Chinese, Malays and even the British ... their women stay by their men. In fact, there ... the men are the heads of the households, not the women."

His stories and their banter kept them up half the night on most nights.

"Are there any vegetarians like us? What did you eat there?

"Oh, Chellam! The food ... No way, you don't want to be a vegetarian there ... there is so much variety ... there is this Chinese dish – Hokkien mee. It's a noodle dish ... like the string hoppers that you make ... and they add another type of noodle to it ... a thicker one made from rice or wheat flour and egg. The Chinese hawkers fry these noodles with prawns, eggs and pork pieces and wrap it up in a large *opeh* leaf ... do you know what an *opeh* leaf is? It's not really a leaf ... it is actually the bark of a betel nut tree ... and oh, Chellam ... the fragrance that you get when you open the package at home ... ahhh."

He raised his five fingers to his lips and kissed them.

"Nothing in Kerala comes close to it ... why did the Chinese only leave woks and fishing nets in Kerala! They should have left their noodles and recipes here ..."

She was perceptive enough to notice the faraway look in his eyes that kept getting longer and longer. On those nights, she didn't push him any further for answers. Once a man had tasted adventure, there really was no going back.

So, when he broached the topic of returning to Singapore several years later, she wasn't surprised, nor did she have the heart to stop him. He was getting increasingly nostalgic about Singapore and restless in their village. The straw that broke the camel's back was when his maternal uncle refused to allow him to spend his hard-earned money from Singapore on new clothes for his children on Onam day. Everything Krishnan had earned in Singapore had been added to his family's coffers.

By now, she was a mother of three and her youngest was still a baby. There was no question of her leaving with him. Besides, women from her community generally lived in their maternal ancestral home their entire lives with their children rather than with their husbands in separate homes. Her great-grandmother, the matriarch of their family, had done so. Even her mother had done so. Fathers did not always play a big role in their children's lives. Inheritance and descent were traced through females.

There was really nothing she could do, but let him go and fervently pray that he would return soon.

Barely had a year gone by when her younger brother, Sivashankaran, raced home with a Malayalam newspaper in his hands from the tea shop. Chellamma had just gotten all three children to nap when he burst into the room shrieking.

"Japan is going to attack Singapore. *Aliyan* (brother-in-law) can never come back … at least not till the war ends. If he is …"

Their home was mayhem for the next few hours with family and neighbours gathering and contemplating what to do. Some brought news from their relatives in Singapore that they had received in the aerogrammes a few days before.

Someone mentioned that the ship leaving Madras at the end of the month for Malaya was the last one for now, as the route was getting too dangerous. No one knew when travel would resume between the two countries.

Others said that the Japanese troops were no match for the British soldiers who were far bigger and stronger.

It was then that she said the words that changed the fates and lives of her descendants forever.

"I have to go to him. Come what may, in good times or bad times, my life is with him!"

It was an unusual stance to take for a young woman in her late twenties from a respectable Nayar family. But they were at the brink of changes that were sweeping across Kerala. Ancestral homes like theirs were beginning to crumble around them in the face of reforms to inheritance and marriage laws sweeping through Kerala.

Maybe her great-grandmother too recognised that things were changing in Kerala. With so many of the men leaving for jobs overseas and rejecting the old ways, there was a concerted push to change their customs. Or maybe, she recognised the look in Chellamma's eyes.

"Let her go! Send Krishnan a telegram. Send the boys with her too … just in case … they can look after her and help with the children."

The matriarch of the house had spoken. She ruled the home of fifty-eight extended family with an iron fist. No one disobeyed her – not even her older brother.

She then took her oldest grandson's hand and half-dragged him out to the garden behind their home. It was clear to everyone where she was headed. The matriarch was leading Gopalan to the serpent shrine – the home of the guardian and protector of their ancestral home. Several members of the family followed them. It was an important moment. No one from their family had left the country before.

This time – in a much calmer voice – she addressed her oldest grandson. "Gopala, promise me in front of our serpent shrine that you will bring Chellamma back to this land safely after the war. You know that she's the eldest of the cousins … one day she will run this home. It's her duty. And when she does, she will need you by her side to help her. Promise me that both of you will come back."

One did not renege on a promise made at the serpent shrine. Everyone knew that.

Soon, arrangements were made for them to leave her village and the country for the first time. They booked a second-class cabin on SS *Rajula*. It was comfortable, with four bunk beds, and they could even bring a servant boy along for free if they wished. They passed off their sixteen-year-old brother, Sivashankaran, as one. But the journey itself was debilitating. Chellamma found that she had to care for four seasick "children", including her teenage brother and deal with the impending danger of getting caught in the crossfire of the war.

So, it was a relief when the captain announced that they had reached the shores of Singapore. Her children ran amok on the ship's deck screaming away pointing to the island in the distance, "Amma … Maama (maternal uncle) … Amma … look … *Singapur … Singapur…*"

Frankly, she could not make out the figures on the shores. All she knew was that there was one more hurdle between Krishnan and her. The ship stopped short of docking at the harbour. She watched in horror as the crew threw rope ladders down the sides of the ship and instructed all passengers to disembark quickly into the waiting boats.

No one on board seemed to protest. Everyone was all too eager to escape the ship and get to the safety of the shore.

They say love gives you strength. Love and her Guruvayurappan (her favourite deity) gave her strength that day to climb down the rope in her sari whilst clasping one child in her hand and coaxing the other two to move slowly to the waiting boats, ready to take them to the shore. Her brothers handled their luggage.

Then she saw him. There he was in the sea of men, standing taller than everyone around him, with his signature broad smile and holding a bunch of lotus flowers in his hands.

As soon as they stepped onto the shore, her daughter, Devagi, dashed towards Krishnan's outstretched arms. Chellamma smiled as she watched Krishnan bend over, ready to hug his daughter. But for some reason, both of them fell to the ground. Next to her, Gopalan too tumbled to the ground and as he did, frantically stretched out his hand to her. Chellamma saw Devagi yell out and Krishnan falling on her. But she could not hear the screams. All she could hear was a sharp ringing in her ears that would not stop and that she would never forget in her lifetime.

The Japanese had dropped a bomb on Keppel Harbour – merely a stone's throw away from where her family stood.

AUTHOR'S NOTE

In our family, stories about strong-willed women who were a force to reckon with are bountiful.

My favourite is of my paternal grandmother, Chellamma Amma, who had told her family: "Come what may, in good times or bad times, my life is with him." It is said that with those words, she packed her bags and her three young children and travelled by road to Madras (now Chennai) from Kerala and then by ship to Singapore just on the brink of the Japanese invasion of Malaya. We believe she was on the last ship from Madras just before the war started. Unable to stop her from leaving, the family had sent two of her brothers with her to Singapore. That much is true.

The story, "An Unusual Arrangement", itself is fictionalised. I have taken the artistic license to imagine what my grandmother's life would have been like in the 1920s based on what I have heard. My grandmother was a brave soul who defied tradition and customs to remain married to my grandfather, Pozhikkara Vaazhavilla Veedu Balakrishnan Pillai. You see, the Nayar community (amongst others in Kerala) are traditionally matrilineal. They lived in an ancestral home made up of members who descended from a common female ancestress. The system was intended to protect women and provide them with a home as the men in the community were conventionally in the military and as such often absent or dead. The matriarch was the head of these homes and ran it with the help of her brother or the oldest male. The relationship between a brother and sister was perceived to be far more sacrosanct than the one between husband and wife. Maternal uncles were responsible for the upbringing of their sisters' children.

Husbands visited their wives in the evenings and returned home at dawn. Although the relationships could be for life, there was no stigma to changing partners if either party wished to do so. Their marriage (*samanthams* in Malayalam, meaning union) itself was a simple ceremony comprising the husband giving his wife a sari/cloth. Matriliny started fading out around the 1940s in Kerala.

In Singapore, my family lived in Sembawang and my grandparents had four more children, including my father. They finally returned to India in the mid-1970s. But they were not welcome at either of their ancestral homes, as no one was willing to share their portion of the property. Not one to be defeated easily, my grandfather built my grandmother a one-storey home in another town called Paripally and named it 'Happy Villa'. My grandmother outlived her husband by about twenty years and passed away peacefully when she was eighty years old in 1992.

Her younger brother, Sivashankaran, migrated to the UK in the 1970s. Gopalan, who had grown increasingly desolate waiting for his sister to agree to return home with him, finally left Singapore in the 1960s and cut all ties with the family. The last they had heard was that he was working as a mandor at Nam Heng Estate in Johor, Malaysia. But despite their best efforts to contact him, no one heard from him ever again. Gopalan's only wish, to keep his promise to bring his sister, the rightful owner of their ancestral home, back to Kerala, was never fulfilled. Little did he know that Chellamma did return to Kerala several years later – albeit without him.

HOW I MET YOUR MOTHER

FELIX CHEONG

Move, damn it.

I was willing the hands of my watch to move faster. It was just about, nearly, almost, close to, borderline-but-never-quite seven o'clock.

Bloody hell. Time sure knew how to take its own sweet time.

Peter saw my face, tense like a hawk waiting for its breakfast to weaken and die. He laughed and gave my left shoulder a light slap.

"Relax lah, John," he said, leaning in for a light on his second 555 stick. "The sun's not even fully awake yet."

Peter was one year my junior, probably had more carbon in his lungs than a man twice his age, and was my best friend as far back as our first fight at five or six years old.

Freddy, my brother three years below me in the family tree but behaved like he had already climbed higher, joined in the ribbing. Exhaling so slowly you could practically count each molecule of smoke, he said, "Yah, she's coming lah. No girl would want to miss your ogling."

I winced. How right he was.

To the untrained eye, we were nothing more than three ruffians, in our tight shirts and drainpipe jeans, hanging around outside our kampong off Geylang Lorong 3. Three goons with nothing else better to do than shoot the breeze with cheap jokes and even cheaper cigarettes.

In truth, we were three boys recently released by the starting gun into adulthood: Peter, to a motorcar workshop opposite Gay World as a mechanic; Freddy, to an office in Collyer Quay where he held a job as a clerk or something equally mind-numbing, and me to Times Printers where I had begun my apprenticeship as a printer.

This was our morning ritual set into motion not long after we declared ourselves independent by virtue of our monthly pay cheque. Freddy and I would bounce out of bed at six and down a quickie breakfast of bread and *kaya*. Or sometimes it was just a cup of *kopi* equivalent in acidity to Ma. We would take care to Tancho down our hair in front of the mirror till we looked Elvis-calm and felt Presley-collected. Then we would rendezvous with Peter here for our obligatory puff.

And watch half a dozen kampong girls on their saunter to the seamstress factory down the road.

In that daily parade of skirts, I would pick her out immediately. She wasn't outstanding because of her height – she was at least a head shorter than me – or hair (thank goodness she didn't spot the beehive that was the buzz around town). She wasn't talkative, smiling quietly at the banter between her friends. And most of all, she wasn't flashy; a simple top and matching skirt would do. Whether polka dot or floral, solid colour or striped, it didn't matter, because her taste was just right, and the whole getup would be held together by a black belt hugging her slim waist.

And yet, she was all that my eyes zoomed in on and paid attention to. Maybe it was her high cheekbones or the shape of her lips. Maybe it was the story in her eyes or the gentle slope of her body. Or maybe it was that gait that made no attempt to exaggerate her curves. Whatever it was that didn't call attention to herself, I was besotted.

There was a moment last week when she had turned to me as she walked by, caught my eyes in the fullness of their longing, and blushed – or what I thought was a blush.

It was like a scene from a Patrick Tse movie. You know that awkward moment when the boy first locked eyes with the girl and the music swelled to the beat of their heart? Yes, *that* moment in *that* scene. Except that I never quite followed through on the script.

I couldn't, and I shouldn't.

Who was I anyway? I was just nineteen years old, still rough around the edges. Not much of a looker, not much of an education either. No real prospects, no real future, as Ma would have me know a couple of times a day; just a job that paid $100 a month to get my hands blackened by day's end, printing newspapers I could barely read from cover to cover.

It was Peter, sensing I had already dipped my toes into that muddy pool called Love, who asked around the kampong for her name. And the grapevine promptly resounded with an answer: Ah Ting.

Ah Ting. What a good old-fashioned Hokkien name, so becoming of a girl so understated. Ah Ting. Ting, ting, like a bell that would wake me from dreams into the sharp light of morning. Or the diffused glow of the future.

Even though she and I were practically neighbours – she was living at the furthest end of the kampong – I had never seen her before. It was a small community – thirty to forty households at most – so it still baffled me why I had not met her before.

"Why don't you tackle her?" Peter said, shaking me out of my reverie. I craned my neck, waved at the *makchik* next door who was dragging her two unwilling children to the Geylang Serai market.

Where were the girls? They were usually not this late. I would have to leave soon to catch the bus to Times House. Kim Seng Road was a good forty minutes away.

"I think Ah Ting likes you!" Peter continued. "She's wearing red every day. Now, what does that tell you?"

"Yah," Freddy said. He had the annoying habit of picking up conversational crumbs from Peter. "When girls wear like that in the office, I also want to tackle! Don't give chance!"

I leaned towards him with my good ear. "Give what?"

"Don't give chance!" he repeated. He was used to my condition, the result of Ma slapping me so hard when I was thirteen years old – for steal-eating a leftover slice of fish in the fridge – that it permanently damaged my right eardrum.

I shrugged. They must have left for work much earlier. Damn it.

Just as I was to give up hope, Hope came along.

And today, Hope was wearing all red, as she had done the past few days. Maybe Peter was right. Maybe it was a signal. A hint of permission to approach her, a red flag that fluttered in the wind to get me all worked up and going.

She looked at me again. And smiled. A curl of the lips, ever so subtle. But a smile it was.

I was too shocked to return the compliment.

★ ★ ★

Move, damn it. Make a move, John.

But I couldn't, for the simple reason I was on the night shift, which began at 8pm and ended after 4am, for the next two weeks.

I had never been on cloud nine before. But throughout that fortnight, there was no other way to describe my light-headedness. Because I got home almost at dawn, I could not hang out with Freddy and Peter for another glimpse of her.

Still, I was feeling heady, fluff following the flow of the wind. And wherever it blew, there I would drift.

It was so distracting I almost lost the tip of my right middle finger because my hand had moved slower than the paper cutter. I just managed to pull it out in time. That was a close call.

Even Ma noticed something was different – or amiss. In the middle of a long-winded nag – it was typically how she unwound after work – she stopped in mid-sentence.

"You been taking *ganja* or what, smiling like an idiot?"

I pretended not to hear what she said, but still nodded. With Ma, anything other than a "yes" would have been summarily taken as defiance.

"I don't know what kind of people you mix with outside. You and that useless boy Peter will never amount to anything," she said. "Not like Freddy. See, he's so smart he can get an office job in town. What good are you? I should have laid an egg and eaten it with soya sauce instead of giving birth to you."

And so it went, round and around. None of it was new, of course. The family story, told and retold till it was an article of faith, was that a few years after I was born, my father had a stroke and passed away. He had just successfully crossed the threshold of forty. Why Ma hated me and not Freddy, I'd never know. And Ma, widowed at thirty-four, had never forgiven me for what she thought was the bad luck I had brought.

Before her tirade could permit itself another breath, I escaped into my room, sat on my bed, wistful.

Ah Ting, Ah Ting. What was she doing now?

"We have an idea!" Peter said when we met again two weeks later. We were doing our best to stay cool – no, look cool, which was more difficult, given we had no money – despite the heat. I was back on the day shift, listless and restless. Maybe it was the two cups of *kopi* I had had to tune my body back to daylight hours, aching in areas I didn't know before.

The airy-fairy feeling was still there, like my head was inside a bubble inside another bubble. Even though I knew where Ah Ting lived, I still couldn't work up the courage to walk up to her doorstep and ask her out to a tea dance. Or a movie at Odeon. I wouldn't know what to do with a "no" for an answer.

"We have a plan," Freddy said. "We came up with it yesterday. But first, one cigarette each to thank us."

"This had better be worth it!" I said.

Just as I surrendered my 555 pack, a sudden confluence of events happened.

First, I saw Ah Ting and her friends ambling towards us. My heart leapt. She was all giggles, more chatty than usual and, more importantly, still wearing red. And she waved at me. A slightest flick of her right wrist.

A good sign, definitely.

Just as I was about to wave back, a blue Volkswagen that smelt of old money made its way down the narrow *lorong* and stopped in front of the girls. From where we were perched on the railing, we saw a young fellow, probably a couple of years older than me, chatting with Ah Ting. She laughed, waved goodbye to her friends and got into the car.

Not a good sign, definitely.

Peter and Freddy looked at me with concern. Even their cigarettes stopped exhaling. You could hear the whole universe drop.

Without another word, I stormed off to work. That was that.

The talk around the kampong the next few weeks was the General Elections, which would eventually propel a certain Lee Kuan Yew to power. I didn't pay it much heed. None of us were old enough to vote anyway, though the possibility of independence was all Peter could talk about as we made our way to the community centre, where we were minutes away from our riskiest adventure yet in our short life – learning Mandarin.

It was all to please Freddy who had recently told us, long and loud – within earshot of the whole kampong, in fact – about a sweet girl in the office he had a crush on. "But she speaks only Chinese," he said, his eyes faraway and dreamy. I recognised that look straightaway.

It was a dangerous situation to be in – I had almost lost my middle finger to a machine because of it. By then, I had already stilled my heart and given up on pursuing Ah Ting. That bubble inside my head had been painfully pricked by a Volkswagen-shape pin. She was clearly out of reach and out of my league. There was no way in heaven or hell – and the many worlds in-between – I could compete with a rich man's son.

"The three times I tried to make small talk with her," Freddy continued, "it was like a chicken talking to a duck."

We empathised, of course, as smoking buddies were wont to do. So, without giving the matter another thought, Peter and I signed up for the evening class too. After all, to know another language was to avail ourselves another hook to bring the fishes in.

Imagine my surprise when we settled down to our seats at the back of the classroom. Five rows in front of us, in a sleeveless top and a pencil skirt, all elegance and grace, was Ah Ting, with four of her factory friends.

Five of them, pretty in a row.

The snigger from Freddy and Peter, when it was obvious my jaw couldn't drop any further, gave the game up.

"We didn't take your cigarettes for free, you know," Peter said in a hushed voice as the teacher, who looked as formidable as the Great Wall of China, came in. "We told you we had a plan!"

"What?" I said, barely able to pick up his whisper.

Ah Ting must have heard the commotion. She turned and smiled, ever so gently.

And for the first time, I smiled back. In that flash, I was Patrick Tse, as the music inside my head began.

AUTHOR'S NOTE

The story of how my parents met in their youth was only revealed to me at my Dad's wake. All along, my parents had told me they had grown up in the same kampong in Geylang Lorong 3, but the finer, juicier details of how they had dated were modestly whitewashed as "like that lah".

It looked like a backstory Dad would take to his urn (and Mom too, for she also succumbed to pneumonia three weeks later), until Uncle Peter showed up at the wake. One of Dad's oldest childhood friends, he regaled us that evening with the amusing tale of my parents' courtship. Instantly, I recognised in it the framework of a rom-com:

Boy meets girl. Boy falls in love with girl. Boy loses girl. Boy gets girl.

What I didn't include in the story is that Dad still didn't muster the courage to approach Mom even though they were now attending Chinese classes together. So, Uncle Peter and Uncle Freddy had to go one step further: they asked a mutual friend, who was good in Chinese, to write a letter to Mom, purportedly from Dad (I believe they must have learned a trick or two from Cyrano de Bergerac). This letter was then left on her desk.

Dad was surprised when he received a letter from her a few days later, saying, in no uncertain terms, that yes, she would love to go out with him. The rest, as they say, is my family history.

However, I had cut off this tail-end of the tale because I felt that the character was coming across as too passive, that inertia had gotten the better part of him and if he still needed another push from his friend and brother, then he probably wasn't really interested in her in the first place. Which was far from it.

The young man in the blue Volkswagen is entirely fictional, although Mom did tell me that Grandma (my great-grandmother) had wanted to matchmake her with a rich man's son. But she, like Dad, was rebellious (they were, after all, baby boomers and the flower power of the 1960s was beckoning) and took to each other instead.

In fictionalising my parents' love story, I had retained its essence but, with the creative licence afforded to a son and writer, embellished it with humour which I hope would do their memory justice.

A PERANAKAN LOVE STORY

JOYCE TEO

★ ★ ★

"Ah Cheng! Ah Cheng!" exclaimed her school mate Gek Neo, "you are going to be late for your first job if you spend so much time dolling yourself up!"

Ah Cheng turned around while trying to get her *kerosang* attached properly on her *kebaya* and smiled. "Don't worry, Gek, I will be ready very soon. It's only a short trishaw ride away, lah!"

As Ah Cheng adjusted her best *sarong* and *kebaya*, preparing herself for her first job, she was both nervous and excited. She was one of the few Peranakan ladies who had a chance for an education in her time and she chose to do a subject which was very different from what the other Peranakan children chose to study. She had enrolled at the new Nanyang Girls' School in the city and studied Chinese.

Most Peranakan ladies from good families would have studied English at the time, in the hope of getting a good government job under the British colonial government. But Cheng, always the rebel, went against the tide. She signed up for a boarding school and chose to study Chinese. Now that her ten years of studying was completed, she came upon one of the few jobs which a lady from a good family could do: a teacher.

Born into a poor family with too many girls, Cheng's biological father decided to give her away to a cousin's family who did not have daughters and welcomed one into the family. The Seah family was better off and was able to give her a better life and an education. Ever since Cheng was a toddler, she had lived with the Seah family as one of their own. In those days, there was no such thing as legal adoption, but Cheng was given the Seah surname and that was the name she had lived with all her life. However, she never forgot that she was adopted and yearned for freedom

When she was old enough to go to school, going to boarding school was one step towards freedom from her adopted family. It was a terrifying time for her at first, living on her own with other students. And she didn't know which was more terrifying: the teachers from China or the ghosts haunting the school! Nevertheless, she survived school and was ready to see the world, earn her own living. The Nanyang Girls' School, being one of the elite schools at the time, often received enquiries from wealthy families looking for private teachers to come to their homes to teach the children in their household. This year was no different and as Cheng was one of the top students in the school, she was selected to be the Chinese tutor for a Teo family living in the Balestier area.

By the time she was ready, the trishaw was already waiting at the gate of the school. Adjusting her glasses, her hair and her best outfit, she took a deep breath and got on board.

The trishaw took about half an hour to leave the city and soon Cheng found herself in a quiet private housing estate in Balestier. As the trishaw got closer to the house, Cheng got more nervous; the houses here were huge! And they were headed for the biggest mansion in the area. As they got to the gate, she noticed that on the pillars on both sides of the gate was the name of the mansion, Wan Qing Yuan, in Chinese characters. She was able to read it, of course, and translated it as "Peaceful Gardens".

An *amah-chieh* in white top and black pants scurried out to open the gate and the trishaw driver pedalled under the enormous porch. Cheng got off as gracefully as she could and waited at the open entrance. The trishaw driver informed her that he would be back in two hours to pick her up and as he pedalled slowly out of the gate, Cheng heard the *amah* calling in the house, "Boss! The new Chinese tutor is here!"

Soon, an imposing gentleman in a Western-style suit and moustache came to the door. "You must be Cheng, the Chinese tutor." He looked her up and down and must have been satisfied with what he saw: a slim, geeky-looking young lady in a *sarong kebaya* and glasses, with her hair up tied in a neat bun. "Come in and take a seat. I will get the children."

Cheng sat at a huge round marble table, waiting nervously. Soon, she could hear chattering and an assortment of children came in. There were ten of them, ranging from about six to twelve years old. Cheng was barely eighteen years old herself, so she felt quite intimidated.

"Allow me to introduce the Teo children and grandchildren," the gentleman with the moustache said. "These are my children as well as those of my brother." As it turned out, it was a huge household. The head of this household was a Mr. Teo. He lived here with his wife and children and his younger brother and his family. The Teo family was well-known in the business world, being involved in various sectors from banking, to farms in Malaya and import of grain from China.

"We are a Teochew Peranakan family and most of the boys study in English schools," Mr. Teo senior explained. "I wanted the younger lot to learn Chinese so that they can continue to do business with our comrades in China."

Cheng nodded. "I will do my best, Mr. Teo." The children were active and voracious learners. They spoke a mix of Teochew, English and Malay among themselves and with their *amahs*. As Cheng was also from a Teochew Peranakan family, she was able to communicate with the children in Teochew and Malay to start with.

To begin their Mandarin lessons, she first taught them to write their names in Chinese and pronounce their names in Mandarin. She also read to the children the various calligraphy works around the house and explained what they meant. It was very enjoyable and a change from the quiet and strictness of the boarding house where she lived.

Very soon, two hours passed and it was time to leave. As she was waiting at the gate for the trishaw, she saw a tall young man, not much older than her, striding towards the house. He was wearing a policeman's uniform. He stopped at the gate and called out a friendly "Hello" in English. Cheng replied shyly in Mandarin. "Oh, you must be the new Chinese tutor my father was talking about." He spoke in Teochew and Cheng replied in Teochew, "Yes, I am. I enjoyed my first day teaching the children."

"Ah, I can tell from your accent, you are Jio Peng Teochew like us!" the young man said. "My name is Nee Wan but everyone calls me by my English name Ted or Teddy."

"My name is Sye Cheng, but you can call me Cheng,"

"Nice to meet you, Cheng," Ted said, as the trishaw pulled up. "Hope to see you again!"

"Goodbye!" said Cheng as Ted helped her into the trishaw and it pulled away.

"What a friendly young man!" Cheng thought to herself. "Pity he seems more fluent in English than Mandarin. He looked very smart in his uniform, though. I wonder if I will meet him again…" Lost in her thoughts, Cheng looked forward to her next lesson with the children, and to meeting young Ted again.

One week flew by, and Cheng was back at the Teo house, waiting to be let in. The children welcomed their young tutor with enthusiasm and the lessons got underway. There was a stack of plain paper and pencils on the table which she assumed were for the Chinese lesson. So this time, Cheng not only read them the Chinese calligraphy, she also got them to learn to write some simple Chinese words. Soon, the children quietened down while they tried to write some Chinese words, giggling when they could not get the strokes right.

Two hours passed by very quickly and it was time to end the class. As she walked to the gate to wait for the trishaw man to pick her up, Cheng found herself looking out for young Ted at the gate. And right on the dot, she spotted him walking up the road. He looked like he was in a hurry but when he saw her, he slowed down and a look of relief fell across his face.

"Hello, Cheng, nice to see you again! How was your Chinese lesson today?" asked Ted.

"It was very enjoyable, the children are so nice!" she replied shyly and felt a blush moving up from her neck to her face.

"Haha, wait till they start fighting! They create an absolute racket!" he said with a smile. He was obviously very fond of his younger siblings and cousins. Cheng was taken aback by how the smile changed his face when he talked about his cousins. His face lit up and he looked quite handsome, especially in his uniform.

As the trishaw man appeared down the road, Ted took a step closer to Cheng and asked in a very serious tone, "Next week, my uncle has organised a *wayang* performance for the people in the neighbourhood. Would you like to stay on after your Chinese lesson to watch the *wayang* with us?" He looked so earnest, she could not possibly turn him down.

"I will have to ask my principal at the boarding school but I am sure it should not be a problem for me to stay out a bit later next week," she answered tentatively. Besides, she was curious now and interested to find out more about Ted and his family.

"Tell her one of the Teo brothers will personally escort you safely back after the show. I am sure she will allow it!" Ted called out as the trishaw went slowly down the road and Cheng waved her goodbye.

When Cheng returned to the boarding school and told her friends and the principal about the invitation, there was a buzz of excitement. The young female boarders could not stop talking about it. The Teo family was one of the wealthiest in town and most had not even been to that part of town, let alone the mansion!

The principal was not too sure at first. She was afraid that a young lady all alone at a *wayang* performance was not quite appropriate and could somehow get herself into trouble. As they discussed the matter in her office, the principal started to realise that this might not be such a bad idea after all. And when Cheng told her that one of the Teo brothers would personally escort her back, her eyes lit up. "The young policeman?" she asked. "Yes," Cheng replied. "Well, in that case, you have my permission," the principal replied and added, "By the way, could you see if his father and uncle are willing to donate some money to our school?"

"Yes, ma'am," Cheng replied and rolled her eyes as she left the office. "Ah, so that is why the principal is keen for me to socialise with the Teos!" she thought to herself.

On the day of the *wayang*, when Cheng arrived at the mansion, she was surprised to see that the grounds were totally transformed. There was a *wayang* stage at one end of the garden, benches were arranged in front of the stage, small lights were hung all around the ground and at the other end of the grounds under the porch was the biggest *tok panjang* she had ever seen. *Amahs* were hovering around the table setting it up for dinner.

As to be expected, the children were distracted. They could not stop talking about the *wayang* which was happening that night. So instead of trying to get them to read or write, Cheng decided to tell them some legends from China which are usually performed in wayang. She ended her stories with *The Butterfly Lovers*, a tragic love story of a pair of lovers, Liang Shanbo (梁山伯) and Zhu Yingtai (祝英臺). By the time she ended her story, the children had tears in their eyes and as she looked up, she saw Ted at the entrance of the house, looking quite moved himself.

As she ended her lesson for the day and the children ran off to get an early dinner, Ted came to the table and sat next to her. "That was a good story, beautifully told. I wish my Mandarin was more fluent," he said in an admiring and wistful tone, casting his eyes her way.

As Cheng looked away, not wanting to come across as too forward, Ted cleared his throat. "While the *amahs* prepare the *tok panjang* for dinner, would you like to have a look around the mansion?" he asked. "Yes, please," replied Cheng shyly as Ted stood up and showed her the way out of the room.

The house tour was fascinating, not just because it had so many interesting artefacts scattered all over, but also because Cheng got to enjoy the stories Ted told her about his childhood growing up in Wan Qing Yuan.

She found out he was twenty-four and the second son of the first wife of Mr. Teo's younger brother. His father had two other "junior wives" and the word around town was that he was looking for wife number four. He had many brothers and sisters and several half-brothers and sisters.

While he was quite high up in the hierarchy of the household, with the younger ones calling him "Second Brother", Cheng learnt that the Teo wealth would go to his oldest brother, the first and eldest son, Reggie.

The family had enough businesses and income such that his father did not have to work a day in his life, and Ted knew that if he was so inclined, he need not work as well. But knowing that he was not going to inherit any of the family wealth, he decided to go against the grain and get a government job with the British colonials. As he was tall and well-built (he and his brothers loved body building), he ended up getting a job as a policeman, which caused quite a stir as most of the family members worked for the family businesses, if at all.

From listening to Ted, Cheng started to admire his determination to make it on his own and saw in him a kindred spirit.

After the tour, they adjourned to the *tok panjang*, which, by this time, was filled will huge platters of food. Cheng was so impressed with the large bowls of *bakwan kepiting* soup and platters of meats and seafood cooked with *rempah* to the *buak keluak,* which had a deep dark colour and the most wonderful aroma. It was obviously the most popular dish as the guests were digging in and enjoying the meat, gravy and black nuts. Cheng found out that this dish alone took more than two weeks to prepare as the *keluak* nuts were poisonous and had to be soaked in water and washed daily for two weeks before they could be cooked and eaten. What Cheng remembered was that it was the best Peranakan food she had ever tasted.

Apart from the delicious food, the evening was quite confusing, as Ted tried to introduce her to all the Teo family members and their friends. Cheng did not remember everyone but Mr. Teo, Ted's uncle, appeared to know her family, the Seahs, and was nodding approvingly. Mr. Teo was particularly interested in finding out if Cheng could help the family understand their ancestry in China by writing down their family names and ancestral village. Mr. Teo explained that since most of them had studied in English schools, they were no longer proficient in the Chinese language, but he was keen to return to his ancestral village one day.

After dinner, Cheng went off to watch the *wayang* with Ted and his family. She impressed them by helping with the translation of some of the text as the actors spoke in classical Teochew, which not everyone could understand. And what do you know, the story for the night was *The Butterfly Lovers*!

Cheng had the most memorable time that night and when Ted dropped her off, using the family car, the principal was waiting at the entrance of the boarding school. She bowed low and shook Ted's hand enthusiastically, telling him about the fundraising drive for their school. Cheng tried not to look embarrassed while Ted politely said that he would mention it to his uncle.

After that night, Cheng would meet Ted after her weekly Chinese lessons with the children and she would also help him privately with his Chinese language. She wrote down the Teo ancestral village name for him and passed copies to his uncle and brothers. Soon, she became an important part of the family as, young and old, the Teo family would consult her whenever they needed help reading any Chinese document, from the *tong shu*, or Chinese almanac, to announcements in the Chinese newspapers and writing letters in Chinese.

As Cheng and Ted got to know each other, their love grew and a year later, Ted, the handsome Peranakan policeman, asked Cheng, the bespectacled Peranakan Chinese teacher, for her hand in marriage. By then, Cheng knew Ted was the man she was meant to marry and she said yes without any hesitation.

AUTHOR'S NOTE

This story was inspired by the love story of my paternal grandparents. This rebel couple got married and moved out to make a home for themselves in Johor. After having six sons and two daughters, they moved back to Singapore in their retirement years with their eldest son, my late father. I never knew my grandfather well, as he passed away when I was very young. I only have a few photos of him carrying me as a child and looking very happy but frail. I am the first child of his eldest son, and the eldest Teo grandchild of his bloodline, so he was understandably a doting grandfather. However, he passed on too soon.

My grandmother lived to a ripe old age and I used to love listening to all her stories of the good old days. This short story was inspired by all the anecdotes told to me by my grandmother. My grandmother was the one who shared with me where our ancestral village was in China and wrote our family names in Chinese. A few years ago, one of my aunts decided to get the Teo clan together and we started work on our family tree. We have since traced our family all the way to our first ancestor, Teo Lee, who settled in Singapore. That was when I became interested in our family history. Sadly, my grandmother had dementia during her last years and passed away before I could ask her more questions.

I was particularly taken with the stories of my great grandfather with his four wives and his successful businessman brother who supported Sun Yat Sen and whose mansion in Balestier was used as a meeting venue when Sun Yat Sen was in town and is now a museum.

   As I was writing this story, I was moved by the fact that my grandparents were kindred spirits in that they went against the norm in those days and made it on their own, rather than expecting to live on the family wealth. As a fresh graduate, I used to wonder: if we had such well-connected relatives, why did we not ask them for help? Once I asked my father and he told me: just like him and his father before him, we can always make it on our own. There is no need to seek help from others. We never spoke of this again. Now, I understand.

DELIVERY

Yeoh Jo-Ann

★ ★ ★

Eastern Daily Mail and Straits Morning Advertiser
January 28, 1933

Don't all step up at once, ladies, but there's a chance for one of you in Penang.

The following advertisement appears to-day in the *Penang Echo*:

> Wanted:
> A wife; must be good-looking and young.
> Interested parties please apply to FCH, c/o *Penang Echo*

In connection therewith the Editor writes: –
Penang mothers need no longer ask what to do with their girls, as an advertiser in today's *Echo* wishes to find a wife. We, however,

implore applicants to reply by letter, as the members of our staff unfortunately have not been given authority to judge applicants for the post. We are considering barricading our doors if merry maidens in search of a husband storm Beach Street tomorrow.

———

The Penang Echo
February 14, 1933

Chap Goh Meh Reflections, by D. Young

To-day Miss Modern is no longer in need of the once-popular custom of local girls going to the river side and throwing oranges into the water to enlist the help of the deities in their matrimonial ambitions. Miss Modern, no longer the shy *nyonya* of her mother's generation, turns up her nose at the need for a third party. She is perfectly capable of direct negotiations.

The modern Penang girl no longer peeps at you through the chink in her door as you pass by her house. You no longer have to wait for Chap Goh Meh to see the young lady of your dreams. She will walk on the Esplanade whenever she likes, of her own accord, unaccompanied except by perhaps a servant, her pretty face exposed to the vulgar stare of strangers.

A certain Miss L was spotted on such a stroll just last week, a whole seven days before last evening's traditional annual excursion of Penang's fine young ladies. Even if one were to ignore the bobbed hair (so many ladies have succumbed to this in the name of fashion) and the lipstick, one could not ignore her shoes. They seemed to be made of or covered with feathers or some other unsuitable material, and so high it was a wonder she managed to move at all.

Even last night, amid all the hubbub of Chap Goh Meh, as every eligible maiden of the best Chinese families went out to the Esplanade to see and be seen, Miss L and her shoes tried their best to steal the show. One wonders if, unlike her sisters, Miss L seeks to eschew her maidenly status not for a matronly one but for something more ornithological? A magpie, perhaps.

Do I speak for the island's *babas* when I say I miss the self-conscious girls, the *sarongs* and the *kebayas*, when I long for the glorious days of sweet *nyonyas* with their hair in *sangguls*, balancing crowns of *bunga burong* of hundreds of gold and silver birds studded with tiny diamonds? Instead, we must content ourselves, and contend with, the modern misses, all ready to shave their heads if fashion demands it.

Miss L will, of course, have shoes to match, if such a thing comes to pass.

––––––

February 15, 1933

My dear Ting,

Was that your sister they were talking about in the *Echo*? Delicious. I would love to see those shoes. Perhaps you will bring her with you when you and the baby come over for tea on Sunday?

Yours ever,
Mrs. Amelia Chan TS

P.S. It is ever so strange and wonderful to be able to call oneself "Mrs.". But I suppose you will laugh, having done this for two years now.

P.P.S. It *is* strange and wonderful, even if you do laugh!

<u>February 16, 1933</u>

Dear Amelia,

It is just like you to be curious about those dreadful shoes, but my sister must not be encouraged. My father is still furious about the article and my mother has turned down all of next month's invitations, except, of course, for the Khoo wedding. Poor Mummy continues to hope that Qwee will end up with the eldest Khoo son. But what would a man like Khoo Chiang Leng want with my sister? Who has, by the way, cut up the article and stuck it to her wardrobe mirror.

Dear Mummy can always hope, I suppose.

On Sunday I shall bring, instead of Qwee, the photographs that Kiam Peng has sent from England. He appears to be enjoying his time at Cambridge.

Yours,
Yeoh Ting Ean, Mrs.

P.S. It's perfectly acceptable for young brides to be thrilled at being able to call themselves Mrs. I myself may have found it a source of excitement for one or two weeks.

<u>February 18, 1933</u>

Dear Mr. Young,

I read with equal parts amusement and despondency your reflections on Chap Goh Meh four days ago.

I am in complete sympathy – the modern misses to-day need a lesson or two about dressing and behaving like ladies. My students at the Anglo-Chinese Girls' School are no exception. I have often had to lecture the school girls about talking as if they were in a coffee shop and not a classroom.

It was easy to surmise that the Miss L, of whom you speak, is one of my former students, Lim Qwee Ean. A most disrespectful girl, and she always found a way to make the uniform fit her, if you understand my meaning.

I wonder sometimes if we are mistaken in trying to give these local girls an education.

Regards,
P. Brooke

February 20, 1933

Dear Mr. Young,

I have decided to address my letter to "Mr." Young because you must surely be a man.

I feel I must inform you that we are living in changing times, that to-day women in Malaya may be called to the bar in England as well as here in our own country, and that you must accept this, whether or not you are inclined to think of it as a step forward for society. You would also do well to accept the other horrors you expound on at length in your melodramatic piece in the *Penang Echo*: bobbed hair, lipstick and outspoken ladies are here to stay.

As for shoes, perhaps you would prefer it if we all returned to binding our feet – that would certainly make us easier to *contend* with.

Sincerely,
Mrs. B. H. Oon
Lim and Lim, Advocates and Solicitors

———

A sign on Kimberley Street:

> Sing & Son
> Elegant shoes for every occasion

Handwritten sign posted on the door, February 20, 1933:

> We regret we **do not** make feathered shoes. Kindly enquire elsewhere.

———

A notice on the door of the *Penang Echo* offices on Beach Street, February 23, 1933:

> Re: Wanted: Wife, January 28
> The advertiser seeking a wife is no longer accepting applications. The *Echo* will not enter into any correspondence or discussion on the subject.

———

February 25, 1933

Miss Lim,

    I have finished your shoes.

    I have also finished the book you lent me. It is good. Many times I used the dictionary. Thank you for the dictionary. There are parts of the book I cannot understand, but it is a good book.

I hope to see you soon. Good-bye. Thank you.

Sincerely,

F.

———

February 27, 1933

Dear Kim Foong,

You were right, as always. The shoes look much better in green than in red. I really should have listened to you from the start. Grass, you said, not fire. You were so right!

Oh, the shoes really are divine.

But I am dreaming already of another pair! I've made a few drawings. On Friday, I shall bring them (and those biscuits we like) to the shop and we can talk about it. I couldn't sleep last night from thinking about the shoes. Do you ever feel like this?

My sister has thrown out her old copies of *Vogue*, but I have saved them for you.

Yours,

Qwee

———

March 1, 1933

Dearest Kiam Peng,

I hope your studies are going well. We all miss you, especially me and Mummy. Our father tells everyone that you are at Cambridge (he says Camp-breej, but no one seems to notice) and he put all of the photographs you sent us of you and your friends on the college grounds on the coffee table in the front parlour to-day when Aunty Beebee came by the house with *kuih bahulu*. (They were delicious – I wish we could send you some.)

Unfortunately, Aunty Beebee also brought a decidedly un-delicious morsel of news. It turns out that Qwee has been teaching Old Liang's son to read. Why it would occur to our sister to teach a shoemaker's son to read in English, no one knows, but according to Aunty Beebee's band of gossips, it has been going on for an indecent amount of time. Mummy assumes this means a month, but I suspect it is much longer. He's been making her her ridiculous shoes for nearly a year now, I believe. I knew it was a mistake for our parents to indulge her in this ridiculous hobby. Can it be called a hobby? I find it is more like a haunting. She spends days and days – and sometimes weeks – drawing the most unseemly shoes and then that man makes them for her so that she can make a spectacle of herself.

I suspect the man has social ambitions. But I am surprised to find that he has managed to compel our impatient, unteacherly sister to teach him English. It must be the shoes that he's using as currency.

Our father has decided that his favourite daughter is being the compassionate creature he always assumes she is. Honestly, if she wanted to wear trousers, he would let her, saying how wonderful it is for her to want to understand the differences in men's and women's clothing. Mummy is scandalised and now talks of nothing but getting Qwee married off to the eldest Khoo boy. Try not to scowl when you read this; instead, you must wish us luck. Just think how much better it will be for her to be safely hitched to your school-time rival than gallivanting about with riffraff.

Do write soon, as I am already impatient for your reply. Can you send me a few copies of *Vogue* with your next letter?

Your loving sister,
Ting Ean

———

March 5, 1933

Dear Miss Lim,

I hope you are well. I hope you will come to the shop soon. I have biscuits for you. Tea also I have, always have tea. We can eat biscuits and drink tea. I will show you my drawings and we can go to my friend's shop to see ribbons. He has very nice ribbons.

I hope ~~you will come I will see you~~ you will have a nice day. I am sorry this paper is dirty. It is tea. But I have drawn a bird here for you because you like birds.

Sincerely,
F.

———

March 8, 1933

Dear Kim Foong,

I'm sending over this note with a stack of drawing paper. I've packed it in some old clothes and told Ah Meng to be very, very careful to avoid puddles as she cycles to your store. I hope you will find this a joy to sketch on, as I do. And if you run out, I will get you more – so you must not try to save it, as I know you will.

In any case, paper as good as this deserves drawings as good as yours and not my poor scratchings. Do you know I keep an album of all of your drawings? I must show it to you sometime.

My favourite is the one you made on that cracker box some weeks ago, the one of the roses. When I look at roses now, I think of your drawing! Of course, I saved that one as well.

I'm busy this week helping Mummy with errands. She seems to suddenly have so many things for me to do. Perhaps it's this upcoming wedding at the Khoos'. Weddings are difficult for Mummy; they remind her I'm not married and may never be. Why doesn't anyone ever ask me if I want to be married? I'm sorry if I sound like I'm in a temper. I'm not. I've just been wanting to say all this for a long time now, and it's coming out in this letter to you.

I will see you soon and we will go look at those ribbons, yes, we will.

Yours,
Qwee

The Penang Echo
March 17, 1933

A Little Shangri-La …

… is what you get when Mrs. Khoo Ai Ling and her clan pull out all the stops for the first wedding of this generation. Anyone worthy of an invitation to the Khoo house on Macalister Road last night found themselves in a lamp-lit wonderland of caged birds, exotic linens and lush foliage, with silverware-laden tables set up in the back garden and swaths of fabric chasing one another through the branches of the trees overhead.

The bride, formerly Miss Khoo Gaik Eng and now Mrs.

Chan, was stunning in an intricate gold head-band and a gold-embroidered cheongsam tailor-made in Hong Kong by, of course, Moon Kee. The mother of the bride was resplendent in coral, in a cheongsam made by the same illustrious tailors. Guests arrived in assorted finery, with many of the ladies sporting organza dresses with quivering puffed sleeves a la the lovely Joan Crawford in *Letty Lynton*. One lady stood out among these gauzy beauties: Miss Lim Qwee Ean, the eldest daughter of Mr. Lim Kek Seng of Lim Textiles, who wore a sleeveless, full-skirted sapphire-blue dress with a trail of mother-of-pearl buttons down the back. The dress ended just above her ankles to reveal shoes made of overlapping strips of jade-green silk that curled upwards and outwards like so many blades of grass. Mr. Khoo Chiang Leng was overheard to remark to the bridegroom, Mr. J.P. Chan, that Miss Lim appeared to have brought her own garden with her.

This would have been apt, considering that his mother had brought one of her brother's restaurants, the Pearl Phoenix, to the party, with the staff operating out of the Khoos' own kitchen. Guests were treated to all the delicacies Chef Wong is so well known for, including his specialty, Nine Treasures in a Pond, for which our Governor is reported to have a regular craving.

Beauty, food, jazz, dancing – it would have taken a stone not to be entertained last night at the Khoo residence. Certainly one for the books!

March 18, 1933

Dear Pamela,

I expect that by now you must have seen the article in the *Echo*. My mother is furious. One little sentence on my cheongsam, on which the tailors will probably dine for a year, and so much drivel on those silly shoes! My brother is amused. Of course he is – the article makes Chiang Leng sound like some witty Clark Gable type, when he's really just a dressed-up bookworm.

Did you happen to speak with Miss Lim at the wedding? Isn't your sister Amelia good friends with her? I really must find out who makes her shoes. Do you think it could be someone in Hong Kong? Or Shanghai? I find it hard to believe that anyone in Penang could contrive to make such shoes.

Yours,
Gaik Eng

March 19, 1933

Gaik Eng darling, hope you'll like the cake – very buttery, one of Mother's best. And since Ah Yong is taking you this note, he might as well bring something to distract you with as well.

Because no, I didn't speak to Miss Lim at the wedding, and no, my sister is friends with her sister and not her. Qwee Ean was in the year above mine at school, though, and really rather funny. She once glued the Geography mistress to her seat! Mrs. Brooke was fuming for days.

An idea: why don't you invite her to lunch or something, and see if you can pry details of her shoemaker from her? If anyone can, you can.

Kisses,
Pam

———

March 21, 1933

Dear Miss Lim,

Will you come for tea on Saturday? My mother and I were entirely charmed by you last weekend at the wedding, and she desires to meet you in a more intimate setting.

Yours with warm regards,
Mrs. Chan Gaik Eng nee Khoo

Attached, a handwritten card:
Mr. and Mrs. Khoo Phoon Huat request the pleasure of Miss Lim Qwee Ean's company at afternoon tea on Saturday, March 27, 1933.

Four o'clock, at their home at 300 Macalister Road.

———

March 23, 1933

Dear Mrs. Chan,

Thank you for the kind invitation. I gladly accept and look forward to seeing you and your parents on Saturday.

Yours,
Miss Lim Qwee Ean

Eastern Daily Mail and Straits Morning Advertiser
March 25, 1933

Appearing to-day in the *Penang Echo*:

> Wanted:
> Capable shoemaker of ladies' shoes. Must be skilful with leather, silk, feathers.
> Please apply to ABC, c/o *Penang Echo*

> Wanted:
> Designer of ladies' shoes, with knowledge of European fashions and ability to work with various unusual materials, including feathers and stones.
> Interested parties may apply directly to Sing & Son, Kimberley Street.

The Editor adds: Much, much ado about shoes – this seems to be the season for outrageous footwear, with young ladies all over Penang clamouring for the title of Best Shod and even established purveyors beginning to cater to this newfound taste for impractical shoes. If this continues, we may find ourselves compelled to divert all Sports pages to Fashion. Gentlemen, for all our sakes, we implore you to reason with your wives.

March 27, 1933

Dear Miss Lim,

I hope you are well. I hope you will come and try your shoes. I have finished. I hope you will like them.

The magazines are very nice. Thank you again. For the paper too, thank you. I am sending you a bird.

Sincerely,
F.

March 29, 1933

Dear Miss Lim,

It was a pleasure to meet you again on Saturday. I was at the bookstore today and recalled you mentioned wanting to read this book, so I hope you will accept it as a gift.

Please convey my regards to your parents.

Regards,
Chiang Leng

March 31, 1933

Dear Mr. Khoo,

Thank you for the copy of *To The Lighthouse*. How very kind. My parents send their regards.

Yours,
Miss Lim Qwee Ean

April 3, 1933

Dear Miss Lim,

I hope you are well. You have not come to my shop. I saw you and Ah Meng at the tailor shop but you did not come to my shop.

I hope you will come soon. I send you another bird.

Sincerely,
F.

April 5, 1933

Dear Kim Foong,

I'm really sorry. Last week, I was asked about the wonderful "grass" shoes you made for me, but I could not bring myself to tell anyone your name or where the shop is. I hope you will not be angry with me, though I am a bit angry with myself. I have been quite, quite selfish and I'm ashamed.

Thank you for the bird drawings. They are beautiful.

Yours,
Qwee

April 6, 1933

Dear Miss Lim,

I am not angry. I am sending you another bird.

Sincerely,
F.

April 8, 1933

Dear Miss Lim,

How nice to chance upon you today. It was a pity you were in a hurry to get home and could not stop to talk, but I hope you will accept my mother's invitation to lunch this weekend. I look forward to seeing you again.

Have you finished the book?

Regards,
Chiang Leng

April 9, 1933

Dear Mr. Khoo,

I have finished the book, and I wondered what to make of the ending. A woman with an artistic vision? I suppose Mrs. Woolf was referring to herself. She certainly wasn't referring to anyone I know in Penang.

Well, at least we are still allowed books. Thank you again for the thoughtful gift.

Yours,
Miss Lim Qwee Ean

April 11, 1933

Dear Miss Lim,

This time I am sending flowers. I find that the best books have difficult endings, or endings that make me struggle to accept them.

I hope to see you at lunch on Sunday.

Regards,
Chiang Leng

April 18

Dear Kiam Peng,

Writing this postcard in a hurry. You will never guess what has happened. Mummy has just told me that she and Father have received a proposal from the Khoos. Just this afternoon! Khoo Chiang Leng and our Qwee! Mummy is so thrilled.

Qwee has been surprisingly quiet and she's been shut in her room for hours now. It is just like her to be dramatic about this.

Ting Ean

The Penang Echo Weddings & Engagements
June 9, 1933

The wedding of Mr. Khoo Chiang Leng and Miss Lim Qwee Ean will take place this Saturday, the 14th of June.

June 30, 1933

Dear Kim Foong,

My turn to send you a bird. What do you think of the drawings? Do you think you can make this?

I'm sorry about last week. I didn't mean to cry. I really mustn't. Everyone, especially Mummy, tells me how lucky I am. It's funny, I think, that everyone feels they must tell me how lucky I am to be married and settled and finally have a husband. No one ever asks. Except you. Which is why I howled like an old ghoul, instead of saying thank you for asking like I should have. I hope I didn't frighten you too much. I really am feeling better now.

I'm doing more drawings and will bring them when I can. My mother-in-law entertains nearly every evening and it is hard to get away. I don't know how Chiang Leng puts up with it, but he manages to look interested in everything these people say, even if he thinks it's all terribly silly and tiresome. He says it is all part of being in business. I think I shall stick to drawing.

People keep asking about the shoes, all the shoes. Especially the ones you made for the wedding. Are you really sure you don't want me to bring them all down to your shop? They will all want you to make them shoes, and then you'll save enough to move to Hong Kong and set up a shop there, like you've been dreaming of.

Yours,
Qwee

July 2, 1933

Dear Madam Lim,

Don't bring these people to my shop. They will be sad and I will be sad. I cannot make your shoes for them. Without you, shoes like that cannot happen.

You remember, when you first came into my shop. You said to me, I want my feet to look like fish. First time I heard anyone say this. You drew a shoe and then you drew fins, a tail, on the shoe. And I wanted to make this shoe. I wanted to try to make the fin and the tail, but also the scales. I started to think about colours, about how fish look like while they swim. You and me, we fought and fought, but we made nice shoes. You still have the fish shoes? They are still my favourite.

Maybe the new bird shoes will be my new favourite. Your drawings are good. Swallows are graceful birds, but you have also made them look playful. I will think about how to make the shoes.

Please come and drink tea with me when you can. I have nice biscuits.

Sincerely,
F.

P.S. Is it correct to use "Madam" Lim? The tailor says you are keeping the name Lim.

July 21, 1933

Dear Pamela,

We are going to finally find out who my sister-in-law's mystery shoemaker is. I overheard her telling Ah Meng, her maid, to watch out for a parcel to-day, and I am certain they will be shoes. Qwee thinks of nothing else. My mother thinks she is quite mad, drawing shoes and strange-looking plants and animals all the time and taking long walks with her maid everywhere, but my brother is quite besotted with his wife. Fool.

But you know that – you saw what he was like at the wedding, making moon-eyes at her. My mother said it was quite indecent. I thought her *shoes* were indecent. What kind of bride wears shoes like that to her wedding? Glass slippers! (*Were* they actually glass? Mirrors?) The woman thinks she is Cinderella. I think she is pathetic.

Anyway, to-day I'll sneak a look at her package when it arrives. There's bound to be a label or a card.

Yours,
Gaik Eng

July 21, 1933

Dear Madam Lim,

I am sending you the bird shoes. Maybe you will come and have tea next week if you like them. I thought of you while I made them. Sometimes, I heard you talking to me, saying I must make the wings longer. So I have given the swallows very long wings.

I wish it was as easy to give people wings. I would make myself wings and fly to Hong Kong. If I make you wings, where would you go?

Sincerely,
F.

July 22, 1933

My dear Ting,

I was hoping to call on you, but my mother-in-law has suddenly decided that my sisters-in-law and I must learn to make some sort of jam, so this note must do instead.

It's to do with your sister. I don't know all the details yet, but I think you should know that she's in trouble. Her sister-in-law, Gaik Eng, is friends with my sister, who dashed over here this morning to tell me that it's all chaos at the Khoo house because they seem to have intercepted a secret correspondence between your sister and a shoemaker on Chulia Street and they suspect the unthinkable. Honestly, it sounds like a tawdry romance novel, but it must be so very terrifying for your sister.

Gaik Eng told Pamela that Mrs. Khoo locked Qwee Ean into the upstairs bathroom while she and the maids searched the bedroom. Goodness! In the middle of it all, Chiang Leng came home and roared and let her out. I don't know what's happening now, but she's not allowed to go anywhere now and they may send her home, even if Chiang Leng is against it. Oh, Ting, I hope not. That would be too awful, it really would.

Yours,
Amelia

July 14, 1933

Dear Kim Foong,

I've asked Ah Meng to explain to you what has happened. I want you to know that I have told them it was always me who sought your company, who badgered you to look at my drawings and make my shoes. It was I who kept all the letters and the drawings, after all.

I don't know what else to tell you because I don't know what I will do. Whatever happens, I hope we will meet again.

Yours,
Qwee

July 20, 1933

I have been thinking of Hong Kong. We should go together.

Q.

July 30, 1933

Dear Mrs. Khoo,

Your husband came to see me last week. He has a kind face. He said he wants me to know he loves you very much and he will do anything for you. You should let him.

I am sorry. One last pair of shoes I have made for you. My friend who sends fish to the Khoo house will take this letter and the shoes to Ah Meng. Dragons will protect you and bring you luck. I hope you will sometimes remember me when you wear them

Your friend,
Kim Foong.

July 31, 1933

I am coming to see you, later. I have news. Please wait for me.

Q.

August 2, 1933

Dear Kiam Peng,

I am afraid I have terrible news. She has disgraced us all. I can hardly believe it, but it's true. All this time, Qwee has been carrying on with her horrible shoemaker, and now she has run off.

Mummy has locked herself in her room and our father hasn't spoken since we heard the news yesterday from the Khoos. Chiang Leng assured us that he would keep looking for her and that he will tell us if he hears from her. Poor man. He looked so lost. I felt so sorry for him; even Mummy waited until he had left before she became hysterical.

I heard that Mrs. Khoo found a whole heap of love letters in Qwee's wardrobe. Is that why she taught the man to read, so he could write her sordid things? I expect she must have been bored, and she thought it was all very risqué and dangerous to dally with someone of that class. Shocking, even for our sister. To risk such a good marriage, with such a fine man and a fine family! The shoemaker – what did he think would come out of this? I went to the man's shop to demand an explanation, but it is all shut up. I think the Khoos have run him out of town, or he has heard that they will and decided not to wait for the axe to fall.

Aunty Beebee has just arrived. How quickly these vultures catch the whiff of disgrace! I hope this does not damage my chances at being elected Secretary at the Ladies' Garden Society.

Your loving sister,
Ting Ean

August 3, 1933
The Penang Echo

Missing – Khoo Bride Disappears

A month and a half after her wedding to Mr. Khoo Chiang Leng, the new Mrs. Khoo, formerly Miss Lim Qwee Ean, has gone missing from the Khoo residence on Macalister Road. She was last seen by the household staff on the evening of July 31 and was reported to be in perfectly good spirits. Mr. Khoo Chiang Leng, her husband, has declined to speak to the *Echo* on the matter, as have his parents, Mr. and Mrs. Khoo Phoon Huat.

Our police sources confirm that a report has been filed on the younger Mrs. Khoo's disappearance and investigations are being carried out.

Mr. Lim Kek Seng is offering a reward for any news of his daughter and her whereabouts. Applicants may go directly to Lim Textiles, Burmah Road.

August 5, 1933

Dear Pamela,

That woman is the very devil!

Chiang Leng has been very stoic about everything. He packed up all her things himself. Mummy thinks he's given them all to the poor – but what would the poor do with shoes like hers? I wonder if he will tell me where he's put the shoes. Especially the swallow ones. When he saw those shoes the shoemaker made for Qwee Ean, he said, he knew he would never have her. How morose of him; perhaps it's all the Russian novels he's been reading. But they are beautiful shoes and that snake of a shoemaker is an excellent craftsman – when I opened the package that day, I nearly cried out. The stitches were so fine, Pamela, and he had made swallows made out of silk and gauze and attached them all over the tops of the shoes, with straps around the ankle shaped like swallows in flight. I was about to try them on but my mother came into the room and I had to explain what I was doing and then we read the shoemaker's note together. It was so horrible.

I have never seen Mother so angry. She will never forgive her for carrying on behind Chiang Leng's back with what she calls a "poor, stupid shopkeeper", so it's a good thing Qwee Ean has decided to run away.

But it would be a shame to waste good shoes, do you not agree? Do you think that if I wait a month and ask Chiang Leng nicely, he will give them to me?

Yours,
Gaik Eng

August 31, 1933

Dear Chiang Leng,

We have arrived safely in Hong Kong. Thank you again for the tickets, for trying so hard to understand, for making all of this possible. Kim Foong and I hope to one day pay you back.

I am so, so sorry for everything, but I hope you know I will be forever grateful, forever in your debt, forever wishing you only the best. I would never have been a good enough wife for you, you know.

One day when we open our shop, the first thing we will make is shoes for you. They will be softer than butter and I will sew birds on the inside. Phoenixes, eagles, kites. Peace, strength, grace.

Good-bye, Chiang Leng. Good luck.

Love, always,
Qwee

To the Lighthouse, 1927
Virginia Woolf

Yes, she thought, laying down her brush in extreme fatigue, I have had my vision.

AUTHOR'S NOTE

My grandmother, Lim Suan Tin, liked to tell me stories whenever I visited her in Penang, about growing up with seven sisters, surviving the Japanese invasion, struggling with marriage, tradition and poverty. I listened to these stories over and over as I grew up, and never got bored of them. But the story of her eldest sister she only told me once, and it felt like she had waited until I was ready to be told of my First Great-Aunt, who was constantly upending social conventions and, in a scandalous turn of events that shook Penang society, ran off from her marriage to the very suitable boy her parents had selected for her. When she told me all of this, my Ah Mah was sympathetic — "My sister was just too modern for our times. People weren't ready for a woman like her."

Except, in a funny way, that very suitable boy. "She was very lucky, you know," my grandmother told me. "He could have made her life very, very difficult, but he chose to help her." I wanted very much to emphasise this — that they both struggled, that they were both brave. So I slipped into my story the ending of one of my favourite novels, *To The Lighthouse*, in which a woman artist finally succeeds in finishing her painting. In speaking of the novel, my characters speak of artistic visions, difficult endings — and this is how their story, and my story, ends as well.

In fictionalising this un-fairytale romance, I pored through old newsreels and accounts of Malayan women, both historical and anecdotal. Chunks of these old articles have found their way into the story, in subject matter (that Chap Goh Meh piece is inspired by a real deal) and in language. My favourite discovery while plodding through newsreels was of B. H. Oon, a Penang girl who became the first Malayan woman called to the bar in England in 1926 and later Malaya in 1927, after the constitution was amended to allow women to be called to the Malayan bar. In my story, I've included a fictional letter from this real woman. I hope it would have amused her.

FRENI'S MARK

MEIRA CHAND

★ ★ ★

Everything of importance happens on a Wednesday. Other people are full of dates, June 4th, March 26th, 1962, 2002. I do not remember dates; I only remember Wednesdays. My mother said I came into the world on a Wednesday. Wednesday's child is full of woe, she remarked, staring at me sadly. Mr. Wadia, the cat, came to us on a Wednesday. He was a scrap of fluff and bone, savaged by crows. The cook found him and would have thrown the kitten out with the garbage had Khorshed not seen him in time. Khorshed was married on a Wednesday. Eventually, she returned to me, as I knew she must, and that too was on a Wednesday. It is only I who know these things have happened on a Wednesday.

★ ★ ★

Mother ran The Coronation Hotel by herself after Father's death. She had no time for me and so I was left with my sister, Khorshed, and the servants. When Mother spoke to me, her voice was without the warmth she showed Khorshed. Introducing me to guests, she thrust me before her, as if surrendering ownership of me.

"This is Freni; she's a little slow. If you speak too fast, she will not understand," she explained.

People smiled then and nodded and began to speak to me in the way I speak to Mr. Wadia. Khorshed never made me feel different, only Mother. She lives in her own world, Mother would explain to guests, even as I stood beside her. I do not feel different. I only feel me.

Sometimes, Mother gave me messages to take to the rooms of guests. She wrote the messages in her sweeping hand on a piece of paper. At the bottom of the page she wrote the number of the room. The paper was soft where it was torn from a pad and, written in curving black letters at the top of each page, was The Coronation Hotel. I could not read the messages Mother wrote, but I recognised The Coronation Hotel, like a bridge across the page, its letters soaring, then dipping. And I knew about numbers. I liked the way they sat beneath the messages, written extra-large for me; 16, 8, 22. I liked their blackness and the way they danced upon the page, together or alone.

Khorshed left me once, before her marriage. She went to look after a sick aunt on the outskirts of Mumbai. Without Khorshed, the great bed we shared was like a vast white field filling the room. I could not sleep while she was away, but remained vigilant, ready for whatever might come. Our home in The Coronation Hotel was full of strange noises, gurgling pipes, running water, the sudden scrape of furniture on a stone floor in a distant room. Sometimes, Mother's voice floated up, far away, issuing orders, talking to guests.

I cried with relief, seeing the clear direction of my life again when Khorshed returned from the sick aunt. Without Khorshed, the world was confusing. I clung to her hand, even through meals, that day she was restored to me. Khorshed laughed but that night in our bed, she found a torch and, in the dark, shone it beneath my hand, lighting up my fingers until they appeared transparent. She took a pin and, on the top of my thumb, scratched the K of her name and, upon her own hand, she helped me incise an F. I slept then, Khorshed's bleeding K carved into my hand.

I wanted the wound to leave a scar and so, the next day, I retraced the K with a pin, again and again. The pain was as nothing when I thought of how I would wear Khorshed's initial upon me forever. There is still a faint white K upon my thumb, but Khorshed's scar disappeared, leaving no trace of me upon her.

Even though Khorshed rescued the cat, he knew it was I who loved him. Khorshed says he is not the same cat but a third or even a fourth Mr. Wadia, but I do not believe her. In the days when Mr. Wadia was a kitten, The Coronation Hotel was a gleaming white castle with green painted shutters. Its gables and turrets, seen from a distance, rose majestically above the surrounding shantytown of that area of Colaba. In the foyer ceiling fans circled lazily above tall green palms in blue-and-white Chinese pots. Ornate mahogany furniture, with the carved feet of lions or tiger's heads, filigreed to a thick brown lace, stood about the foyer beside small tables with crystal ashtrays and crocheted mats. The black-and-white marble floor resembled the board upon which Khorshed played chess with Noshir Delal.

The same guests returned to us each year on their visits to Mumbai. I remember Noshir Delal, a tall white-haired man with an ivory-topped cane. He told me I was the Red Queen and danced me across the checkerboard floor in a game of fantastical chess, the wild music he hummed vibrating in his chest. He twirled me about and cried, "Checkmate, Freni."

I remember the circular sweep of the polished stairs, slippery as water underfoot, flowing down into the foyer. I held Mr. Wadia tight as I descended, the fear of falling always with me. The delicate clink of china and glass rose up from below as guests sipped on tea or lemonade, turning fans stirred the crystal droplets of chandeliers, hanging on dusty velvet-covered chains. Mrs. Pochkhanawalla from Poona visited regularly, dressed in silks and diamonds. "Come, Freni, sit with me. How is pussycat today?" I remember her diamonds, clear as beads of rain, and her beige lace sari.

Whenever there were messages for Noshir Delal or Mrs. Pochkhanawalla, I ran along the corridors as fast as I could, Mr. Wadia under my arm. Noshir Delal always stayed in Number Four, a corner room overlooking the garden. He offered me sticky mints wrapped in waxed paper, and I sat on a carved chair as I chewed. A Flame of the Forest tree blazed beyond the window, and the room was perfumed by his shaving soap. Those days are gone; that world has vanished. It was Khorshed who killed that world for me. She decided to get married.

His name was Rustom and he was a distant cousin. He came

often to The Coronation Hotel and waited quietly in the foyer for Khorshed to be free of her work.

Once I heard him say, "Tell your mother we'll take Freni with us, then she'll let us go."

And so, it was I who chaperoned them before they were married. We drove out in Rustom's car, I alone in the back seat, they together in front. The car smelled of old leather and petrol fumes, and the seat had a rent through which its insides bulged. As I watched them talking to each other, I pulled at the horsehair stuffing, rolling it between my fingers until my skin was raw. I observed the growth of their relationship, the excitement simmering in their bones, faces full of secrets I could never know. In the back seat, I listened to Rustom's voice, thin as his lips. I sensed then that the love between a man and a woman could never be more than the tyranny of one over the other. There was nothing I could do. Before me, amidst petrol fumes and the strange light in Rustom's eyes, Khorshed was sucked from my life. I have never forgiven Khorshed for choosing so paltry a love as compared to my own.

There was no conviction in her the day she married. Her face was like a pebble under water, sometimes showing clear and sharp, then drowning beneath ripples of uncertainty. The conviction was all in Rustom's face. His teeth gleamed behind wet lips, his eyes were shiny and bulging. He appeared so bright and gleaming I was forced to avert my gaze, anger throbbing through me.

The same fury filled me when their daughter was born. I went to visit Khorshed in the nursing home with Mother. Khorshed lay in a white room upon a white bed, her hair wild against the pillows. The layers of pain through which she had struggled still hung about her. I knew that beneath the sheet she was slack and empty. She had been used, filled and emptied by her husband's wasteful love. I have never felt so sick and angry as I felt upon that day.

They called the child Ava. She was a miserable creature from which there came an incessant whine. If I pinched her hard in secret moments, the whine became a scream.

As she grew, Ava whined and screamed no less than when she was tiny and later, she learned to stick out her tongue at me. All this I bore for Khorshed's sake, for I could see the growing anguish in her face. Her visits to The Coronation Hotel became more frequent, and each time she stayed longer. One day, she did not leave at all, and soon suitcases and boxes arrived from her home in Bandra.

On her return to us she busied herself with the running of the hotel. By then, Mother was old and sick and glad to leave everything to her. I ignored the changes in Khorshed, and the time she now spent with Ava, that before she had spent with me. She was back with me again; nothing else mattered.

At first, I was afraid Rustom would reclaim her. Sometimes he stormed into The Coronation Hotel and I listened to their raised voices as I sat in my room, hands clenched tightly in my lap. However hard Rustom tried to persuade her, Khorshed did not return to him; she chose instead to stay with me.

All these things happened long ago. They are now shadows in my mind. Now, Mr. Wadia is so old his mouth droops open as he dozes on his favourite chair. Khorshed does the same, asleep on a threadbare chaise longue in the afternoons. I sit and watch them dozing together in their separate chairs. Sometimes, I feel I see the cat in Khorshed and Khorshed in the cat. Father is there in Khorshed's long nose and straight brow, and Mother in the set of her eyes. I see Ava in her soft mouth and her chin. Sometimes, I think Khorshed is no more than the bits and pieces of other people, all bound together by Rustom. He is everywhere upon her still, in the tiredness of her face, her greying hair and the bags beneath her eyes full of the tears of her marriage. Most of all, I see him in the raised white stretch marks upon her belly. It is there that she bears his deepest scar, where she stretched herself about his child. It is only I, who love her most, who have left no part of myself upon Khorshed.

Like Khorshed, the hotel has also declined. Now a large sign hangs over the gate, Boarding and Lodging. Reasonable Rates. For some time before she died, Mother lay bedridden in room Number Nine. Khorshed and Ava cried for days when she passed, but I felt little. She died on a Wednesday, that is what I remember.

The decay of the hotel did not upset me as it did Khorshed. Night hid time's worst ravages and in the dark corridors the past overwhelmed the present for me. Sepia engravings still hung upon the walls, depicting temples and hill stations and crumbling forts. They looked no different than when I ran down the same corridors with a message for Noshir Delal.

I did what I always did that day. I fed Mr. Wadia as usual, at four o'clock. Our old servant, Gopal, had boiled Mr. Wadia's fish, and it lay curled in a pan, flesh flaking into the juices about it. The eyes had already fallen out of its head and lay, opaque as pearls, in the

thin gravy. I scooped them up with a spoon and threw them down
the sink. I never allow Mr. Wadia to eat the eyes. I do not want to
think about them inside him when I hold him on my lap. I put
Mr. Wadia down on the table with his lunch.

At the other end of the table was a silver tea set that Khorshed
had found and polished into life. Set out beside it were cups of fine
china painted with violets that I remembered last in the diamond
ringed hands of Mrs. Pochkhanawalla. Khorshed told me in the
morning that Rustom was coming to visit her. He was coming,
Khorshed said, because Ava had got engaged to someone called
Soli. There was a sudden softness in Khorshed's voice when she
spoke Rustom's name.

Mr. Wadia was heavy after his lunch, and his breath was covered
with fish. He did not struggle in my arms as we climbed the stairs
to Khorshed's room. She lay upon the bed, her sari high above
her ankles, and smiled as I entered. All about us in the room was
the ugliness of neglect. The walls were stained with dark patches
of mildew, the furniture was scratched and battered. I could cry
when I remember the splendour of Number Four when Noshir
Delal resided there.

"Ava is going out today with Soli," Khorshed announced as I
entered the room.

Ava sat before the mirror of the dressing table in her short sari
blouse and long petticoat, her midriff bare. A pink sari, ironed
and waiting, was draped upon a chair. Her petticoat was tied
shamelessly low, revealing her navel, which swam like a secret eye
in the middle of her smooth, slim body. Her hair fell in a soft sheet
down her back. Khorshed's hair had once been the same, but now
it was grey and short and coarse in texture. Ava scowled as I sat
down; I know how much she hates me. Her mouth was as big as

ever and her voice was still an incessant whine.

"Before I married your father, Freni Aunty was our chaperone. Do you remember that, Freni?"

Khorshed's voice was gentle with memory but within me, there was only bitterness when I remembered those rides in Rustom's car.

"Come and have tea with Ava and Soli. Go and change your sari, put on something nice. Look at you, covered in cat," Khorshed remarked.

I picked up Mr. Wadia, and turned to the door; yet, even before I left the room, the weight of the future bloomed within me.

"Why did you have to tell her? Why can't she stay out of sight until Soli has gone?" I heard Ava say as I closed the door.

I already knew what I would wear to tea. Mrs. Pochkhanawalla had gifted her beige lace sari to Khorshed, who eventually gave it to me after cockroaches had dined upon it. Such things did not bother me.

I held Mr. Wadia tight as I descended the stairs into the foyer. Now the black-and-white chessboard floor was overwhelmed by a creeping, brown disease, and the damask seat I had once shared with Mrs. Pochkhanawalla regurgitated wire springs.

It was many years since I had seen a strange man in The Coronation Hotel. The brightness of Soli's eyes and his unfamiliar voice made the teacup shake in my hands. Some liquid slopped onto my lap. Khorshed looked at me sharply while Ava stared scornfully at Mrs. Pochkhanawalla's sari. In the light of the foyer I saw that cockroaches had eaten further holes in the lace.

Soli's eyes followed Ava as she poured out the tea. He had the same feverish light in his face that Rustom had had all those years ago. Their eyes exchanged secrets over the table. I remembered the same palpitating expression in Khorshed's face that I now saw in Ava's face. I knew then that the secret knowledge denied me had to do with the touch of a man. My hand began to tremble again, the teacup rattling on the saucer. They turned briefly to stare at me, before resuming their conversation. Khorshed's voice was suddenly loud with excitement.

"It is almost arranged. I know I've sold out cheaply, but I just want to be rid of this place. What will Freni and I do here alone after you marry? I shall take a small flat somewhere near you," Khorshed announced to Ava.

"Daddy's so changed, and he's asked you to go back to him so many times, Mummy. Why don't you ...?" Ava broke off with a giggle as Khorshed smiled coyly.

I put down my cup in shock, rage spreading white hot inside me and, picking up Mr. Wadia, I prepared to go back upstairs to my room. All I wanted was to be free of them, and I could see the relief in their faces as I turned away.

At last I heard them go. Ava and her fiancé went out in a car as Khorshed and Rustom had done, but without a chaperone. Times had changed, said Khorshed.

Rustom came at seven o'clock, but I did not go down to meet him. Instead, with Mr. Wadia, I went to sit in the dark at the top of the stairs where I could watch, unseen. Downstairs, Khorshed had lit the great room with candles, and put a crocheted cloth on the table. She wore an elegant sari of soft silver greys that matched her hair.

Rustom sat with his back towards me. After all these years, I still knew the shape of his head and the way one of his ears stuck out larger than the other. The only difference was that his bald crown now rose above a half-moon of hair, like a polished mountaintop.

"And you think she is happy, Khorshed?" I heard his high voice again.

"They seem suited. I felt both happy and afraid, looking at them this afternoon. I was reminded of us," Khorshed spoke sadly and Rustom leaned towards her.

"Did you think any more about my suggestion? Shall we try again? I have had nothing to drink for five years now. I'm a different man. It is not too late for us, Khorshed." He reached out and took her hand.

I could see the years together in their faces; the things shared and done that nothing could erase. I saw then that in spite of everything, Khorshed had always belonged to him.

When he had gone, Khorshed turned with a sigh to climb the stairs, lifting her sari free of her ankles, humming happily to herself. Her face was suddenly full and soft, the years stripped away. Rustom was everywhere upon her again, even the smell of his cigarettes pervaded her sari and rose up the stairs with her towards me.

I stood up to protest the horror of it and heard a screeching, like the desperation of a trapped bird, and knew the sounds came from my own throat. Khorshed stopped in surprise on the stairs when she saw me. I reached out, shouting, willing her not to return to him, and gripped her bony shoulders. I wanted to shake her like I had once seen Mr. Wadia shake a rat by the neck, until it hung limp in his mouth. Instead, hot tears covered my face as Khorshed pulled away from me.

Balanced on the step below, her eyes were suddenly wide and wild as she tried to clutch hold of me to steady herself. Then she was gone, as if a weight dragged her away down the sweep of stairs. Her sari unravelled, stretching behind her like a streak of silver moonlight down the dark stairwell. Her attempt to save herself had unbalanced me, and I fell forward after Khorshed. One by one, the steps flashed past me, each painfully striking my skull. Then, at last, I lay still at the bottom of the stairs, the pain in my back intense. Khorshed lay beside me upon the chessboard floor, her head loose as a rag doll and at an odd angle, her eyes open and unmoving.

I lay as I had long ago in our bed when we were young, curled up against Khorshed's body, the dark night thick about us. The perfume of jasmine drifted in from the garden and mixed with the smell of warm wax from the candles Khorshed had just snuffed out. If I moved, pain ripped through me, but I knew this agony, like that scar on my thumb, was no more than the mark of Khorshed upon me. Khorshed was mine now, forever.

AUTHOR'S NOTE

The story was written during the time I lived in Mumbai, or Bombay as it was then called, in the early 1970s. I wrote many short stories about India at that time. There is a large Parsi, or Parsee as it is also spelled, community in Mumbai, and this old, orthodox and dying society fascinated me. Parsis follow the Zoroastrian religion, and fled persecution in Persia centuries before. They were allowed to settle in India and adopted the local language and clothing, although keeping their own cultural customs, religious worship, and unique manner of burial. As leaders in industry, science and the arts, they have always been central to the development of India and particularly Mumbai. The powerful Tata family, Freddie Mercury and Zubin Mehta, are amongst many famous Parsis, all from Mumbai. In this modern age the community is an ageing one, and rapidly dying out because marriage with non-Parsis is not encouraged.

Not far from where I lived in Mumbai, was an old, dilapidated but ornately majestic building called The Coronation Hotel. It had clearly seen better days and was run by an aged Parsi family. I used to pass it most days and wonder at its history and the lives and tales within it. This story comes from those imaginings. I never really finished the story properly, and so it has languished, filed away in darkness for decades. I am glad it can now see the light.

PERSONAL

SPACE

★ ★ ★

UNKNOWN TRIANGLE

ROBERT YEO
★ ★ ★

Alice Ho did not tell Rupert Lim about what just transpired. She agreed to go to the Registry of Marriages in the first week of December to register her marriage to him. *But how can I tell Tim at this late stage? I should have told him much earlier ... But I must tell him, I've got to let him know. It will break his heart but ...*

Alice went to the post office and sent a telegram to Tim:

DEAREST TIM (STOP) I AM GETTING MARRIED THIS SATURDAY (STOP) SHOULD HAVE TOLD YOU MUCH EARLIER (STOP) ALICE

★ ★ ★

Timothy Aw was an aspiring jazz composer and saxophonist in mid-seventies Singapore. He worked for the national radio company as a music producer but he was not exactly happy in his job. Although he was told he had a free hand, his feudal boss preferred to air traditional songs from the Western classics or local folk repertoire rather than the Bebop jazz he loved. In presenting his progammes, he had to squeeze in the jazz. *I had to put in Charlie Parker between the pops.*

At thirty, he was also distressed by the prospect of having to enlist for compulsory military training called National Service. He was not particularly religious but he had recently found Buddhism, and realised that one of its major tenets about not killing was strongly pacifist. And to call enlisting a service to the nation was, he thought, especially galling. Also, enrolling would also mean he would have to cut the sixties's long hair he had sported and grown to like.

He thought seriously about migrating to Australia, always praised as the "lucky country". At last he acted, and in early March he went to the Australian Embassy to get a migrant visa form and drafted his letter of resignation from Radio Singapore. An embassy staff told him that to obtain a visa, he had first to produce evidence he has secured a work permit to work in Australia.

The same night he went out on a blind date, forming a foursome. *I have never been on a blind date. I hope she's good-looking.* It was January.

The woman he met for the first time was named Alice Ho. She worked in a bank and she was good-looking and gregarious, fun-loving and willing to spend hours listening to jazz with him. After the first date, they went out frequently, almost nightly, including weekends. They went out to dinners, movies, lounges where he would sometimes join bands whose members he knew and she would join in applauding.

At end March, he told her he had heard positively from both Australian sources. "The embassy has approved my application for a visa to migrate. I'm going for an interview about the job offer tomorrow morning. It's good you agreed to apply for the Australian visa too. If all goes well, we can go off to settle in Sydney together later in the year."

"I hope so," she replied. "Can I get a job there?"

"I don't know. But you have a degree and at your age, it should not be difficult. You told me your bank has a branch in Sydney and perhaps you could ask for a transfer?"

"Ok, I will ask my manager about it."

"Good, it's better to be prepared."

A week later, Tim rang Alice up excitedly as she was about to leave for work and told her he had landed a job. The prospective employer wanted him to leave as soon as possible as there was a vacancy. Later that evening, he explained that, given the sudden development, he would go first, and suggested she could follow after her visa was approved. He was blissful that events had turned rather quickly in his favour and soon he would be a citizen of the "lucky country", with his job, girlfriend and future secure.

Alice took the news with a mix of glee and anxiety. While she was pleased things were going Tim's way, she felt it was all happening too fast, that she was not in control. True, he had thought about her, but she had yet to get her visa, find a job in a new country and make a future with a guy she had known for just three months.

Besides, she had parents she loved as an older daughter and she had not told them about Tim's plans for her. Alice was aware her father and mother knew she had a boyfriend as they had taken his calls occasionally but how was she to tell them that the boyfriend now wanted her to give up her job, leave Singapore and migrate to Australia permanently?

Out with Tim on some weekdays and returning late, she had problems waking up and had to ask her mother to help her. On a few occasions, her mother would nag a little, asking, "Who is this boy you go out so much with? *Aiyoh*, you must like him a lot."

On the April night Tim was to leave, Alice was at Paya Lebar Airport. She was emotionally mixed and he was elated but experienced a niggling anxiety he was not able to shake off. Still, he summoned enough optimism to say to her, "Wait for me but don't mope for me. Enjoy yourself, be active, go out with friends."

"I'll try," she replied weakly.

She did try, but her heart was not into going out. She was deeply split between staying and going. *To go or not to go.* She called the Australian Embassy and was informed her application was still being processed. Tim wrote a couple of air letters to tell her he was staying temporarily in a hotel and slowly settling into his occupation. He repeated, "Go out and enjoy yourself."

On day, she spotted a June issue of *The Straits Times* about an audition for a debut play by a local playwright to be presented by the University of Singapore Society. The playwright was Rupert Lim and it was reported that he has just published a novel.

Alice had always been active in school singing in concerts and acting in plays and decided she would break her isolation, intrigued by the prospect of acting in a "local" play. She rang up the society's telephone number and discovered that the dramatist was a Singaporean and he would be present at the audition. She lit up at the prospect of participating in a vehicle featuring Singaporean characters which was vastly different from the Western roles she was used to, the last being in Chekov's *Three Sisters*. Tim's words recurred: "Enjoy yourself, be active, go out with friends."

To her delight, she landed the lead female role. The story revolved around a group of Singaporean students in London in the mid-sixties learning to cope with a more liberal environment than the one they were used to at home. She landed the role of the feisty young woman who in a careless evening gave herself to an Italian man and became pregnant. The director of the play informed her that rehearsals would start in a week's time and staging in the last week of September at the Drama Centre.

In early June, she received a letter from Tim giving her details of his job, that he had found an apartment close to his office and was slowly getting used to his new life. He asked if she had received news of her visa application and once that came through, he would buy her a one-way air-ticket to Sydney.

She wrote back at once, feeling somewhat guilty as she had not communicated with him since he left. She told him that she had not heard from the embassy. Meanwhile, she had taken his advice to enjoy herself, had auditioned for a stage play and landed the lead role. She had also met the playwright and found him interesting.

Rupert found Alice intriguing. She was lively and talkative, spontaneously responding to last-minute suggestions about things to do. And soon they began to date seriously. Rehearsals were usually from 8-10pm and Rupert would pick her up at 5.30pm from her office and they would go for drinks and dinners and into rehearsals.

Before she really realised it, she found herself in a new relationship without disentangling the ongoing one. As the days buzzed, what with work, rehearsals and dates, Tim became a distant promise and Rupert a close reality. Rupert attended rehearsals as much as he could to see more of Alice. She went through lines with him in the car, deliriously asking if she had spoken the way he had written it. Yes, yes, he purred. After sending her home to Toa Payoh, they smooched in his parked car in the darkness, unable to part.

There was a week's break in rehearsal in August and that gave Alice time to think of Tim. She had not been fair to him, she felt acutely. Though it was not his fault, he was disadvantaged by distance. What was she to tell him? That the visa had not come, which was the truth? That she had fallen for another man, which was also the truth? The first was easy to divulge but the second? As she memorised lines of the play, Rupert became the present promise and Tim the distant one. She began to dread a letter or a phone call from Tim.

In Sydney, Tim welcomed his old schoolmate who had first introduced them in the blind date months ago. He had known of the relationship, that Tim had gone ahead to Australia and Alice was expected to come after. But he had also seen Alice out with Rupert. Singapore is a small place.

He asked Tim, "Do you know that Alice is going out with another guy?"

"No, I don't," he replied, surprised and yet not surprised. "Maybe that's why she has not replied to my letters."

"I heard she's acting in his play," the friend said.

Tim felt like rushing at once to phone Alice and angrily demand to know if she was seeing another man. I should never have asked her to go out and enjoy herself, he thought ruefully. After some time, he decided he would write to her to tell her he would call her on a specific date and time.

Back in Singapore, Rupert's intentions towards Alice took a serious turn. He took her to his home for dinner to meet his widowed mother. On some nights, she stayed overnight. His mother observed, "You are thirty-four already, not a young man anymore. You should think of marriage."

He has been thinking about marriage too and his mother's remark prompted him to think of a proposal. It was one night after rehearsal that he broached the question. She had been expecting it and calmly said she needed time to think about it.

"Why?" he asked gently.

"I am sorry, but I have a history I haven't told you about," she said.

"A history? Can you tell me?"

"Not yet."

Alice tried to feel rationally, if it was possible to be rational about feelings. She was a modern enough girl to sleep with a boyfriend before anything was agreed upon. Her parents would be happy to know that if she married Rupert, they would not lose her to Australia. The visa had not come. Although she had not promised herself to him, Tim had an expectation that Alice had not denied.

The play was a resounding success. *The Straits Times* headlined, "Rupert's play goes off like a shot!" Another reviewer wrote, "Alice Ho's performance was spot-on as the brave but vulnerable heroine in the swinging sixties of London." There were packed houses on all three nights.

Tim's latest letter said he would call Alice on a specific date, a Sunday morning at 11am Singapore time, to talk to her urgently. He asked that she confirm by letter that she would take his call.

She thought about it and decided it was not a good idea. They would both be emotional, she was sure, and likely exchange harsh words on the phone. She wrote back immediately in a short letter to say she would explain in a longer letter what exactly happened. Or find enough courage to telephone or telegram him.

In Sydney, Tim slumped when he received the telegram. He had half-expected it. He did not go into a turmoil, did not go into the blame-game directed at Alice. If anyone was to blame, it was himself, a smart ass who had repeatedly enjoined her to enjoy herself and be active while he was away. He was in the lucky country but his luck had run out. However, his nascent Buddhism comforted him, and he told himself, "It is my *karma* not to have Alice."

AUTHOR'S NOTE

The story is based on a true event concerning my wife and I, and how we met. Names and some details are changed. She told it to me after we were married. We remain on good terms with the Tim character whom I met later, and he had married someone else.

The process had three drafts. The story has been in my mind for a long time, since 1974 when I first heard of it. The first draft appeared as an outline of the story in my autobiography *Routes a Singaporean Memoir 1940- 75*, published in 2011. When Felix Cheong asked me to contribute a story to the current anthology, I said yes, and wrote a first draft. It was largely told in the third person with Rupert as the narrator framing the story. Felix made very useful critical comments, as a good editor should. He suggested that Rupert be removed as the narrator and Alice be given a larger perspective. I accepted them.

I removed the controlling paragraphs of Rupert at the beginning and the end of the tale thereby deemphasising him, centralised the love interest of Alice and Tim, deepening characterisation by giving them some interior lines and exploited irony with respect to Tim migrating to a lucky country. These changes improved the story.

ALTAIR AND VEGA OVER GHIM MOH

LINDA COLLINS

Twilight has come and gone, bringing thousands of chattering starlings which, every evening, nest in trees beside the public housing blocks. The noise before the birds settle is tremulous, and annoying. Not that the birds care. They have been coming here before this place in the western part of Singapore was named Ghim Moh – Hokkien for "golden hair", after red and blonde-haired British soldiers who were once stationed there.

The birds have been coming before any humanoid – Hokkien, Malay, European, Indian, Arabian, Orangi Asli, or Neanderthal – who ever passed here ever named it anything.

They have been coming here from before there was even the idea of names.

Modern human Ellie, of European and Maori descent, stands in the long, utilitarian corridor of her eighth-floor flat in one of the public housing blocks. She and boyfriend Robert – 100 percent northern European – rent it from Singaporean neighbours.

As late-coming starlings arrive and try to find a place in the trees, Ellie is dwelling on past failures, of misfit boyfriends and bad choices. In New Zealand, she fell in with a daredevil cowboy and nearly broke her neck. She lay on the cracked clay ground, staring upward, frightened to move after the fall from a beast. It was the Milky Way above that steadied her, the great wash of the galaxy overhead, the flickering of its stars pulsing their way back to life for her until she could breathe.

Now she is frightened again, more frightened than she has ever been. And so she looks up, once more, for a sign. Across the divide of the Milky Way, the rays of two bright stars blink to each other, telegraphing a connection.

They also send a line of light to Ellie. She wants to reach up, grab it, and float away, as if the line were not attached to stars, but balloons. She recalls the stars as Altair and Vega. Though of course, they have existed even before there was the idea of names, before there was an even an idea of an idea.

To some, Altair and Vega are star-crossed lovers, separated not just by the Milky Way, but by the universe, in a fit of folkloric pique. It's the Romeo and Juliet thing. Altair is a cowherd and Vega, a princess. Once a year, on the seventh day of the seventh month, the universe allows them to reunite, by crossing a bridge made up entirely of birds, for some weird reason. To Ellie, neither astrologically nor astronomically minded, Altair is the questing hero from the *Assassin's Creed* video series. Vega is Suzanne Vega, for her song Luka and its words, "… and they only hit until you cry …", which remind Ellie of her childhood.

And this makes Ellie feel frightened again. What if she turns out like her mother? What if she is incapable of love? What if, what if.

Ellie peers down at a large, white rectangle on the ground, eight storeys below.

It is a newly unfurled plastic thing that will be erected to become a vast tent. The rectangle shimmers in the glow of street-lights. Nearby, smoke rises from joss sticks poked into the earth. People who seem to be of Chinese descent crouch, lighting bundles of coloured paper. It is hell money, fake notes given to spirits as an offering. While Ellie is open to all beliefs, she thinks that her idea of hell would be finding out that in the afterlife you still need money. She has so little of it in real life, as it is.

Yet another worry. Money.

From the white plastic rectangle thin strands of ropes trail like jellyfish tentacles.

Ellie leans over the concrete ledge for a better view. Her blonde hair flops past her face, wind snatching at the tendrils like what an ocean current does with seaweed. Perhaps she is Jellyfish Ellie washed up in Singapore from New Zealand, wanting to link tentacles with the one below. She is Ellie, wobbly as jelly, she is Ellie with jelly in her belly. She is bloody pregnant, that is what she is.

And the baby-daddy, Robert, inside the flat reading or listening to music or just being his cheery chirpy self, is unaware of this. He's the daddy: Is he also someone it is better to leave while the thing in her belly is still jelly?

Robert, boyfriend of six months. Honourable, yet irksome.

He's ten years older than her, desperate to settle down and have a kid to take to soccer matches and see his beloved Liverpool. They'd met at a party. "Why do you love poetry?" he asked, having studied it once at some college somewhere.

Why does she love poetry? Who in their wrong mind could resist such a question? Not Ellie, fed up with failed relationships where she had been deemed a nerd, loopy, too sensitive.

If, in this seventh month of tentative togetherness, Ellie were to tell Robert about Jelly, that she has her own tent and inside its warmth spins a potential person, what would happen?

She can see it. Robert would do the decent thing. He would at once ask her to marry him. He was old-fashioned like that. Would she say yes and the baby be born and they live semi-happily ever after? And if she doesn't tell him, and the flotsam becomes jetsam and she flees Robert because she is terrified of motherhood, what then?

On the floors below, other residents also watch the tent, and the hell money fires. They are people who belong here from birth, Singaporeans, not like Ellie and Robert who washed up in the tropics after drifting in life.

Workmen, perhaps not Singaporean, but cheap labour from next-door Malaysia, haul poles and tent pegs, huge speakers, and makeshift parts of staging.

"It's Hungry Ghost month, hence tent, burning, smoke," says Robert, emerging from the den of the flat. In his working class Northern accent, and ever keen to instruct Ellie as if she were one of his students, he continues, "Locals say that in the seventh lunar month, the gates of hell open and the ancestors come out and chill or ask for money or food and you have to give it to them or they freakin' haunt you."

"Oh, that sounds weird … But what's that got to do with the tent?"

"You can make these ghosts happy by putting on a variety show. That's what the tent is for … Gerrr tie. Dirty *getai*," he said, laughing at his own rhyme. "I've just remembered. That's what the evening is called. I think it's from a Hokkien word, and they do all these cheesy songs to please the spirits and the old guys in the audience."

"Who has the best good time, the humans or the ghosts?" Ellie asks.

"Ghosts, obviously," says Robert. He runs his hands over Ellie's bare arms. She ignores him. What if the neighbours see? Ellie worries she will be regarded as one of those cliché foreigners, flouting the more conservative decorum of this place.

"Ellie, you're in Asia now, people see but don't see. Chill," Robert says.

Ellie hates it when older people say "chill". Like they haven't given her generation enough to deal with as it is.

The rising smoke makes her cough. She goes inside their flat. Robert follows, and raises one finger. "Listen," he says. "It's that next-door neighbour again."

There it is, the repetitive, dragging sound of flip-flops plodding back and forth across linoleum. They had never met this neighbour, just glimpsed the figure of a solitary old man if he left his front door open. He continually paces back and forth across the width of his flat. There seems to be no furniture to impede him. The sound is profoundly irritating.

Robert wears headphones to block it out. Headphones are no escape for Ellie, they hurt her ears. She tunes out the neighbour by thinking of him as a prisoner in a cell, wrongfully convicted of a crime, the injustice of it rendering him perpetually restless. It makes him a romantic hero. But look where romance has got her. Pregnant in a foreign land with a partner who is right for her – doesn't mind her anxiety attacks, likes poetry, hates capitalism – and this makes him about as wrong as could be. She has only ever been accompanied by uncertainty. Imagine loving predictability. It's like imagining Altair as a regular assassin. Impossible.

I am that pacing neighbour, walking up and down under the gaze of my late wife Mabel. She was a singer with the voice of a goddess. How we came to fall in love, I'll never know. I'm just a rough 'n' tumble man. I couldn't keep her in the style she knew, but she never complained. She even sang at the *getai*, to earn extra money for us. Soon, I will see her again. She always visits on the seventh day of the seventh month.

These new neighbours, foreigners, are noisy. The girl is pretty.

Several days later, and the tent is up. Red plastic chairs are being placed in rows. The *getai* will be tomorrow night. Robert tells Ellie they always leave the first row of seats empty, for ghosts. In New Zealand, that would have struck her as strange. Now, she is learning to see this as normal.

Ellie is in the corridor, enjoying the evening breeze. The coolness energises her. These past weeks, she has taken to standing here a lot. It is good to get out of the fetid box of the small flat – no aircon in the living room, only in the bedroom.

Robert, on the other hand, likes the heat, how languid it makes him. Ellie resists being languid. She must stay alert. She is on the cusp of something – motherhood, or flight. "Poor little Jelly, with such a hopeless mum … It might be better if you never come into this cruel world," she tells the evening sky and Altair and Vega.

Robert is immersed in a book, *Siddhartha*. "Are you reading it for the Buddhism and journey of self-discovery, or the lyrical beauty of the language?" Ellie questions him moodily.

Without missing a beat, he says, "Nirvana. I want to know where the band got its name."

Then, turning a page, he casually mentions, "Ellie, I feel like some *biryani*, can you get some from the stall downstairs?"

The request is uncharacteristic. Normally, he would get the *biryani* himself. Perhaps he is trying to be more assertive, sensing her ever-increasing timorousness. Or perhaps he is hungry but the book is so good and he doesn't want to put it down. Ellie agrees to go, she wants to escape the flat. As she shuts the front door, Flip-Flop Man peers out from his security grille. He is in a singlet and tatty shorts. Ellie takes in his gauntness, the hollows of his ribs.

Ellie says a vague hi. He gives a toothy smile, but begins to cough, his body shaking. From his mouth comes a blob of spit. It trembles by Ellie's feet, like a living thing that has emerged from the swamp of his lungs.

The old man is overcome by embarrassment. "Sorry," he says, retreating.

At that moment, Melissa, a Malay neighbour who lives on the other side of their flat, comes out. She is still in her work attire, a blouse with a bow and a tight skirt, with expensive pumps on her feet. Melissa does something at an advertising agency, and is also Robert and Ellie's landlady.

"Hello, Melissa," Ellie says brightly.

"Hi, umm." She has forgotten Ellie's name. The family mostly deals with Robert.

"It's Ellie. I'm off to the hawker centre. Let's get the lift together." Melissa nods, and as they pass the old man's door, where his phlegm lies as a congealed blob, remarks, "Disgusting, isn't it? The neighbour," adding, "he's very poor, you know."

Ellie looks down, unsure of what to say. She has been poor herself at times in New Zealand. Jobs there are hard to get and wages low, so many Kiwis end up going overseas to make money. Perhaps Melissa assumes Ellie is an expat on a fancy salary, but in reality, her life as a relief teacher at a second-tier international school is a far cry from that.

They travel down in the lift. Someone has scratched a drawing of female genitalia on its wall. Melissa seems embarrassed, just like when she saw Flip-Flop's phlegm on the ground, as if she resents these people, her people, and the fact she has to live among them.

When they get out, Ellie asks Melissa, "Going to the *getai* tomorrow night?"

"Not quite my scene. I'm meeting friends at that new café down the street."

At the hawker centre, on a whim, Ellie also buys fried rice for Flip-Flop Man.

Ellie is placing the food packet outside his flat when he opens his door. "For you," Ellie says. She expects that he won't have much English but he says after some initial surprise, "Very kind of you," and beckons her inside. She can't resist a peek. Like theirs, the flat comprises two small bedrooms and the living room, with the toilet and bathroom directly off to the right. For a kitchen, there's a sink and bench. The floor is a faded sparkly green linoleum from the '70s. On the wall hangs a framed photo of an oval-faced, dark-haired beauty in a mandarin collar blouse, singing into an old-school microphone. "My late wife when she was young," the old man says, nodding at the photo. "She was a singer. Would you like some of the rice?"

"It's okay, I've got food for me and my husband," Ellie says, holding up the *biryani* packets, surprising herself by how she had just elevated Robert from boyfriend to permanence. It wasn't intentional. She feels Jelly wobble.

"What sort of songs did your wife sing?" she asks.

"Oh, romantic tunes about the moon and the stars, and broken hearts," sighs the old man.

"That's beautiful, so poetic," Ellie replies as she takes a closer look at the photo. The woman's make-up is immaculate and her eyes seem to shimmer with life. She looks a star, definitely no ordinary singer. It is difficult to imagine her spending her life married to Flip-Flop Man and living so simply in this small flat.

I like this girl. She's not like that Melissa, who looks down on me.

I tell the foreign girl that my Mabel was from a well-off family. I was just a cook for the British Army at the time when we met. She says her father was here with the New Zealand army in the '50s. "Fish 'n' chips, beef stew, fruit cake," I rattle off. She laughs, for such fare is familiar to her, too.

I feel happy to talk like this. Most of my *kakis* are dead. There is no one to share memories with. We never had a child. I find myself telling this girl – Ellie, she says her name is – that for Mabel and me, it was a love match. One look, and that was it. Such things are fated. I want to ask her about her and the man, why do they talk so hatefully to each other, when there is love to be had?

I want to tell Ellie about how wonderful love is when you are in harmony. There is no pleasure in discord. One note can be different, yet it can still complement the other. I was the sound of the earth, of mankind. Mabel was the sound of heaven. Is that too fanciful? I add that although Mabel was trained in opera, she became a *getai* singer to make some extra money for us. She put up with the heat, the noise, her make-up sliding down her face, while drunks harangued and groped her – all for me.

"No wonder the *getai* upsets you," Ellie says. It is not that at all, actually. But there are some things that are too complicated to explain to a stranger.

Today, *getai* night, marks over a month of pregnant indecision. Ellie has still not yet told Robert about the hungry ghost growing inside her. She feels it draining her of energy. Some days, she wants it to just go away. Other days, a spindle is within her, with thread winding on to it, growing bigger. A decision is a loom that will make something material. She is not ready.

She is wandering bare-breasted around the flat and Robert is naked on the couch. Her breasts are fuller already. They look very sexy, but they don't feel like her breasts anymore. Robert pats the couch for her join him. Breasty Ellie and Liverpool playing a match on TV. He will be in heaven.

"Don't you have any ambition?" Ellie blurts out. She didn't mean to, but she is thinking of their future, if there is indeed one.

Robert looks at her for a moment, then asks, "What's got into you?"

"You sit on the couch all the time. All you do is watch TV. I hate ball sports. Don't you see how Freudian they are?"

Robert contemplates this and his semi-erect cock with bemusement.

"Well, I do have ambition, as it seems. My ambition is to take you to bed. And then watch Liverpool."

"Stuff you, Robert," Ellie yells, pulling on a t-shirt. "Stuff you … and your fucking soccer," she says and storms out, banging shut the door as she goes.

Out in the corridor, smoke from the money-burning below has risen and furls around the long space like dry ice. Ellie stops. What has she done? Why is she so angry? Starlings are shrieking their heads off as they plummet to their trees. Flip-Flop Man is pacing.

Robert comes out, adjusting shorts and shirt buttons. He doesn't say anything at first, just stands quietly beside her. There's the slapping of footfalls behind them. "Why does he torment us with that?" Robert suddenly asks.

Ellie feels a peace descend. Perhaps it is because Robert does not seem at all upset. She says, "I don't think he sees it as tormenting us. It's more that he is in his own world. His wife, whom he loved, died long ago and he still misses her very much. I suspect that as he paces up and down, he is talking to her."

Robert gives Ellie the deepest, most loyal look she has ever seen and says, "I wish we could be in love like that."

His sincerity and hope frighten her. But it also makes her feel powerful. That is new.

Altair and Vega smile down on her. Is now the time to tell him? First, a thought-beam must strike her. And it does. To herself, so quietly Robert cannot hear, she says, "Mummy loves you." She says this to Robert, to herself, to her unborn child, and, finally, to her own mother, an alcoholic, who did not.

★ ★ ★

Howling mic feedback sweeps up from the tent into the flat where Robert and Ellie lie on the couch together, bombarded by celestial love-beams. The howling engulfs the apartment block, estate, country, and the universe. Starlings startle from trees, and flee in swathes along star-beams.

The *getai* sound system has come to life. A man tests the mic, reciting numbers in Mandarin, then laughs maniacally.

Keyboards, drums and cymbals hesitantly find their way into a sentimental ballad. The sound is a cacophony. Decibels reach for the sky. Over it all, the emcee gives an introduction, and a youthful female voice takes over. The music bounces into a dance rhythm, and the singer works the crowd between verses, urging "Happy-happy, yor" and the musicians up their tempo.

Through it all, the neighbour's pacing slaps through the walls. Robert covers his ears, then laughs and declares, "Four-four signature time. Both the neighbour and the ballad."

He's right. Ellie stands up, catches the beat, and steps in time to the neighbour's pacing and the *getai* song: eight paces in four-four time. One two three four, one two three four, turn, repeat.

Robert joins her. The predictable beat has a soothing, hypnotic effect. "The old man's got the groove," Robert shouts, and indeed, the timing of the *getai*'s electronic keyboards and drums exactly match the neighbour's footfalls.

The music cuts out. In the silence, the neighbour's flip-flops still keep time. One two three four. Robert hi-fives Ellie, and the music starts up again. Separated by concrete walls but still moving as one, the old man, Robert and Ellie four-time onward.

A while later, Ellie and Robert fall to the floor, exhausted. Ellie wonders if this is the moment to tell Robert about Jelly, but before she can do so, he leaps up, saying, "Why not? Ever since we moved in, I've wanted to play my vinyl at full blast. Led Zeppelin, *How Many More Times*. Let's give the *getai* and Flip-Flop Man a run for their money!"

He crouches at his turntable, and the sound of a bass guitar starts. The walls begin to shake as the bass locks into the driving rhythm of four-four time. Everything is four-four time. "Die die," Robert shouts. "Four four. In Hokkien, the number sounds like the word for death."

"Robert, I'm going to have a baby," Ellie shouts. She wants to banish Robert's words. They could be bad luck. She wants only good things, from right now. She wants to believe in good things so much. Robert turns to her. "What?" And she nods, and he looks disbelievingly at her, and an enormous smile forms on his face.

The *getai* performer ends her song. In the silence, there is the sound of butterfly wings, of old men's frail hands applauding.

"Let's celebrate," says Robert. "How about we go down to the *getai*? That is, if you can, if it's not too much for you and bubs?" This last bit he says, trying it on for size, the concerned dad, and seems to like it very much.

And so they go down to the *getai*. The only spare seating is at the front, with the ghosts. Ellie doesn't care, she has to sit down, her bladder's so unpredictable now. An older woman with a perm and bright lipstick taps Ellie on the shoulder and says, "Just checking if you are a ghost", then turns to her friends and says, "No". Everyone laughs companionably.

A magician comes on, and saws someone in half. Starlings come back to the trees, and light from the moon and the stars falls on the *getai*, the sweating performers, on old faces turned nostalgic, on Robert and Ellie, alive and feeling lucky. Someone sits in the seat next to Ellie. It is Flip-Flop Man, his remaining hair neatly combed back, and actual shoes on his feet instead of flip-flops. Robert glances at him, then reaches over to shake his hand, and Flip-Flop Man responds, holding onto his hand to bring him into his world.

The woman who had tapped Ellie greets Flip-Flop Man with familiarity – "Hey, Ah Niu, come to see some girly-girly?" – then says to Ellie and Robert, "We call him Niu Lang after a love story. See those stars up there," she says, indicating Altair and Vega. "They are a poor boy, our Ah Niu, and a maiden of good upbringing, Zhi Nu, who fell in love. The gods did not favour their union and separated them, but at this time every year, they are allowed to meet for one night.

"Our Ah Niu and Mabel were a love match like in the old story. He was a cook and she was from a good family who disapproved of him, and kicked her out when she stuck by him. So the two of them lived here among us for a long time, till death parted them."

On the seat next to Flip-Flop Man are two red roses reserved for Mabel. He turns to Ellie and smiles, then leans towards her and whispers, "My wife is very glad that you are keeping the child."

AUTHOR'S NOTE

Many years ago I was a young New Zealander who'd moved to Singapore with my boyfriend for work. Money was tight; we weren't expats on fancy salaries. We briefly rented a flat in a government public housing block at, yes, Ghim Moh. Few Westerners lived there. It was exciting being immersed in another culture, but also unsettling. Being away from your home country throws your own identity into the spotlight. Who is the essence of you, without familiar trappings? And who was I, in terms of being half of a couple, a new experience for me?

More than two decades later, I recently visited the flat. It was much the same as it had been. But I was much changed. My earlier self had been someone struggling to love herself, let alone understand romantic love, and confused by what this place Singapore might be. Change began by focusing on the external; making real connections with locals and Singapore culture, be it learning folklore tales from Chinese heritage, or attending *getai* variety shows enjoyed by all races. There was a beauty and decency in this working-class sentimentality that was grounding for me, and I wanted to write about it respectfully. The character of Flip-Flop Man, and his enduring love for his dead wife, Mabel, allowed me to do that, and also to show the universality of romantic hope. The brightly burning stars of Altair and Vega, and their representation as Zhi Nu (Princess or Weaver Girl) and Nui Lang (The Cowherd) in Chinese culture, transport the earthly goings on to the celestial. In this way, I could allow room for a reader to also make their own meaning, be it spiritual, divine, or that of eternal yearning for a loved one. They are all direct lines to the heart.

Oh, and the boyfriend is now my husband.

THE SUN, THE MOON AND SOUP AT IFTAR

NURALIAH NORASID

★ ★ ★

In the many years that they had lived there, Sara's parents had not changed a thing about the four-room flat. The living room walls were still the pink of the viscous Panadol suspension she had been forced to take as a child. Across from her and taking up almost all of the facing wall were the words "In the name of Allah, The Most Gracious and The Most Merciful", the Arabic script embossed in shimmering gold paint upon a black background, the same gold creating a border of geometric patterns around the text. These were all encased in a deep-set art frame of dark wood carved in wreaths of flowers blooming among leaves, with serrated edges and the occasional bunches of grapes and pomegranate.

In a set of display cabinets below it, trophies lined the bottommost shelf, beneath sets of her mother's prized, gold-fringed tea sets and dinnerware. The trophies were mainly from art and writing competitions that Sara had taken part in when she was younger. Some were from her brothers' soccer and air rifle tournaments. At the back, Sara could spot a few of her track team ones, as hidden away as she was after hitting puberty.

Sara's gaze skimmed over the family photographs of outings to the Bird Park and the Zoo, and further to Genting and Cameron Highlands, to rest on the coffee table, on which there were two linen-lined rattan baskets filled with medication – one for each parent, for their diabetes, heart problems and hypertension.

It seemed as if everything about this house was made to make her feel guilty.

From her first appearance at the gate, her father and first brother, who was only a year younger than her and her friend and constant companion growing up, disappeared into their respective rooms. It was not long before Sara could hear the sound of her brother's gaming set-up and the television in her parents' room filter to her in an intertwining orchestra piece of murderous anger, disappointment and admonishment. Her youngest brother, in contrast, had greeted her cheerfully on his way out. He had been going out a lot lately, her mother had told her not long after his steps had gone down the stairs. And in an off-hand way, added, "*Jangan* he bring home a Chinese girlfriend, that's all."

One in the family, married to "one of them", was, in her mother's eyes, enough.

Naqiah, her first brother's young wife, was cheerful too, and met her with a *salaam* and some small talk about the hot weather, as she removed her *tudung*, and about Sara's work at the university where Sara taught cultural anthropology as an adjunct. A conversation that was more of Naqiah going, "Wah, you're so smart" and "You must earn a lot, right", and Sara trying to turn the conversation towards the house – "So clean, so nice, the smell!" – Naqiah's own job; her pregnancy.

Pointing to the growing belly, Sara had asked, "Showing already. How far along?"

Naqiah glowed; touched her belly. "*Alhamdullilah*. Five months already, Kak."

"Naqiah just got back from class at the mosque," Sara's mother said with loaded effusiveness. "She does a lot. Tidy the house. Wash the clothes. Now, cooking and cleaning all she do. Mak can relax already."

The floor was less gritty and the toilets scrubbed Chlorox-scented sterile. Earlier, Sara had gone into the kitchen, sleeves rolled up from muscle memory, ready to scrub at the silicon valleys between the counter tiles and the scratched aluminum of the sink. But she had found them devoid of the black greasy gunk that usually caked them. The fridge was stocked, as usual, but the rubber lining and the trays had been wiped clean. And recently, the whole interior of the fridge smelled mildly of citrus, though there were no lemons or oranges within.

Her mother's voice had floated to her as Sara took in the familiar little containers of fresh ginger, chillis, lemongrass and the lone half-bulb of onion nestled among the eggs, "There is a lot of food in the fridge. Take lah, for Iftar later. Or for lunch, you know, if you not fasting."

Sara closed the fridge door a little harder than was necessary. The dull ache in her stomach reminded her that she was indeed fasting on that twentieth day of Ramadan. That dull ache so early in the day also reminded her that she had not eaten anything during *sahur*, the pre-dawn meal. Not that her alarm had failed to go off, or that she had not placed the dinner leftovers in her fridge.

Not that she had not gone to bed without a *niat*, an intention, to observe her fast the next day.

Not that.

Her alarm had sounded – the chorus to her favourite song from a video game she had loved playing since undergraduate – and she had rolled over and turned it off. She had sat up, looked over at Gary, who was impervious to the alarm, and the weight of the morning. Her gaze caught his large, wide form clearly visible even in the blackout-curtain darkness. His breathing was heavy, broken occasionally by the odd snore or confused mumble. Over it, Sara could hear the low hum of the air-conditioning, and over that, the dead silence of the five-room Punggol flat.

At this particular hour on a Ramadan morning, Sara and her mother would be the only ones awake. Her mother cooked *sahur* from scratch. Usually simple things. Prata, the curry for it from Iftar the night before; fried eggs to go with rice, sweet soya sauce and fresh *chilli padi* broken in two; *cakar ayam*; *bubur – kacang* or *nasi*. Sara would often help finish up the cooking while her mother went to rouse the menfolk. *Sahur* would be consumed without conversation as the sermon from the radio flowed over the dining table in a soft wave of sound. Her father would finish the meal with coffee made thick with condensed milk, flipping through yesterday's *Berita Harian* before getting up to prepare to lead the first prayer of the day. Years of that and Sara would always come to associate *sahur* with the sounds of sizzling dishes, murmuring radio and prayer, and found solidarity in illuminated kitchen windows within a wall of black of the opposite block.

The morning of that day, Sara would have rolled out of bed soft-like, without waking Gary (there was no need to, and especially not after that big fight that they had about religious freedom and respect), but the thought of facing another *sahur* alone, a loneliness that not even the solidarity of neighbouring kitchen lights could alleviate, made her get under the covers again. There, she slipped into a fitful sleep, dreaming of work unending around a warped meeting table scattered with empty documents.

Sara had later left to talk to her mother, or someone about the unease and fear that she felt. The way she prayed only when Gary was not there to see, for fear of it being off-putting to him. About the silence that pervaded her home every morning this Ramadan. About the resentment she felt, that itched like a worry at the back of her head, as she watched Gary sleep in, morning after morning, these past twenty days while she had to be awake at an ungodly hour. The arresting anger when Gary texted, "What do you want for lunch?" or offered her food – biscuits that one time, buns from the bakery, and fruits. When she gave him the side-eye or, much to her chagrin, reminded him that she was fasting, his response was always the same throw-back of his head, face grimacing upwards to the ceiling, followed by, "Ah shit! I forgot!"

She wanted to ask her mother what she ought to do about this. To get answers and validation for the upsets that she felt.

Perhaps, and this she was not willing to think it or accept it of herself, to ask if she had been wrong to marry without her parents' blessings. If this unhappiness that had been roiling in her was a result of that. She had heard so many horror stories about such marriages: adultery and divorces, poverty and death, miscarriages and infertility, uneducated children; every plague-ridden apocalyptic scenario.

But Sara saw that she would never get the answers at her parents' house. She and her mother talked for a while about work and health, about the changes that the family must make to the house now that a baby was underway. Sara kept her eyes on the old grandfather's clock. When it struck, she gave her mother the usual monetary contribution, plus the promise to pay for the housing mortgage and the utilities – something that she had been doing since she had gotten her first job – and took her leave, her heart as heavy and muddled as it was upon her arrival.

Sara did not immediately head home from her parents' home, choosing instead to wander the labyrinths of her childhood neighbourhood. She rounded the green chain-link perimeters of her old primary school, the building which was unoccupied now as it was undergoing the whole school revitalisation project. Conveniently, the temporary holding school was the defunct secondary school that shared its premises, forever gone to a merger.

Sara stared at the primary school building, the new coat of brown and beige dour compared to the green, teal and yellow of the original. The school grounds were quiet, with it being a weekend, eerie as an abandoned palace in a jungle of blocks and open-air carparks with exposed macadam and uneven black patches of asphalt. Sara waited for the wash of nostalgia that never came and left when the security guard finally looked away from his mini-TV to peer out of the guardhouse. Finally, Sara called for a GrabCar via the ride-hailing app on her phone.

It had been a combination of the little things that culminated in that moment in a relationship and she wondered why she had seen the signs and not acted on them. She had friends who ended relationships and engagements just because their partners prayed differently or prayed not often enough. "In the beginning, you always think that you will be okay with it. But the little things add up," one of them told her when asked why.

As she waited for her ride, Sara wondered what kept their

relationship going for as long as it had. They had not been gaming together in months and had other vastly different hobbies. Sara enjoyed quiet, solitary pursuits like sewing and reading, while Gary preferred watching shows and partaking in activities that required going out to places of high activity and strobing lights: arcades, pool halls, bowling arenas.

Her ride finally pulled into view and the driver was thankfully not a talker. So, she was spared having to "Oh", "I see", "Ah!" politely while the driver gave his opinions about everything from the government to the state of the roads. The dull ache of hunger was hitting the level of gastric pains. Sara closed her eyes and let the car radio, tuned then to one of the English stations, fade away into her peripheries. Concentrating her thoughts on things she wished could happen for her – becoming a professor in the university, bedecking herself in battle armour and riding on one of the four horses of the apocalypse (this being of particular interest to her), finally winning arguments against abrasive and ignorant colleagues – she was not even aware when the driver switched to a Malay station, only that he had increased the volume and the voice went from talking about where to get the best *nasi lemak* to the beat of a Hari Raya song.

There was a day years ago when they celebrated their first anniversary together. It was on campus where she had been rushing her thesis to meet the deadline so as to not lose her scholarship. This meant a late day at the Graduate Office. And he had brought her herbal soup. Sara, whose family never had soup unless it was *mee soto* or *soto ayam*, believed soup was not real food but Gary had proudly announced that he had learnt the recipe (that he had "halal-ified") from his mother and this was his first successful pot after several attempts. The liquid was dark and had whole (whole!) cloves of garlic, red dates and wolf berries. And the lotus root was a little like a trypophobic's nightmare. It smelled like a Chinese medicine shop. But seeing how he'd taken the trouble of boiling it and transporting the thermal food container on the long train and bus ride to the campus, one spoonful became another.

In the card that he had given her, he'd written that she was like the sun, always able to warm a room and rake away the cold darkness. Sara was not good with romantic words or gestures. Her idea of romance to this day consisted of getting him doughnuts from Dunkin' Donuts on the way home if she happened to be passing by. So, she told him laughingly, "In that case, you are the moon because you cause waves."

It made no sense, yet all the sense at the same time.

The front gate and door were unlocked and wide open when Sara reached home. Through the entrance, Sara could see into the flat, the walls white because Gary said it made the flat appear bigger and was easy to maintain. Gary would tell anyone who visited that the aesthetic they were going for was Scandinavian, which was all the rage among homeowners their age. To Sara, it was more "Ikea, and Crate & Barrel (when we feel like living it up)" and wore the austerity of two people with full-time jobs and not a whole lot of time to decorate and clean.

Past the bomb shelter and a narrow shoe cabinet-cum-bench, Sara could see directly into the living room. Sparsely furnished: a grey sofa with a mustard throw, a television panel in the same wood as the cabinet, a flatscreen television, a few of Sara's abstract paintings in minimalist frames.

But it was the smell of the soup that caught her when she entered the flat, that medicinal tang from the base ingredients Gary always declared "secret". This was followed by the words of the sermon that would often play on the radio an hour or so before the evening call to prayer during Ramadan. Gary was in the open concept kitchen, all black top on rose-coloured laminated wood, labouring over a pot of the soup on the built-in induction hob. Sara saw that instead of the kitchen island where they always had their meals, the dining table had been set and several dishes were already spread, steam rising from them. There was baby *kailan* cooked with garlic and oyster sauce, steamed tofu in a bed of light soya sauce and a dusting of sesame seeds, and mackerel, fried the way she liked it.

Gary approached her, looking comical in her apron that was too small for him. He wiped his hands on it before he took her bag from her and placed it on the sofa in the living room.

"How's your mother?" he asked.

"She's fine. Managing her health," Sara replied. "You didn't have to cook," she added, turning her gaze away from the table to her husband.

"No lah, it is okay. Simple meal only."

She followed him into the kitchen and stood by as he gave the soup one more stir before switching the stove off. "How did you know which radio station to tune in to?"

"I just tried and tried until this one played," he replied. "I heard it at the bazaar before."

He would not let her help, so Sara turned to getting the drinks from the fridge, where she found a bottle of rose-flavoured *air katira* – her favourite – that sweet, milky drink widely sold this time of year. She wondered where and when he had bought it. And how he knew where to buy it.

When she got to the table, Gary was just setting down a large bowl filled to the brim with soup.

"How many more minutes, *sayang*?" he asked as he started to untie the apron strings.

Sara knew this. "Two more minutes."

"Okay, I wait with you." And then he smiled and opened himself to an embrace.

Gary smelled familiar. His old navy t-shirt smelled of garlic (whole cloves thrown into the pot like some culinary heathen), fried fish and sweat. He had grown more rotund over the years and had taken to calling his belly the "husband belly", just a rank below the "dad bod". Sara closed her eyes. They had always greeted each other with a hug, save for that one time really early in their relationship when he had asked her for one and she had given him two brotherly pats on the back instead. They stayed that way, Gary not asking her why, or saying a word, until the sound of the call for *maghrib* prayers filled the boundless room, signaling the end of the day's fast and a wanderer's way back home.

AUTHOR'S NOTE

Relationships often come with the necessity of navigating the waters of communication and miscommunications, of learning sometimes rather unexpected and unpleasant things about one another, and of accepting those very particularities and idiosyncrasies as part of the fully-realised human being that is one's partner. For interracial and interfaith couples, this navigation is made harder by additional challenges and complications or complexities. When one partner is from a deeply religious background, for example, that may come with the even greater challenge of taboo, societal judgment and even estrangement from one's family.

These are the various facets that I had to consider for my story. During a particularly self-reflective moment during the month of Ramadan, the protagonist finds herself reconsidering her relationship with her husband due to what she is beginning to see as fundamental differences in their values and belief systems. (To be honest, how many of us can say that we have not been a little miffed when we have to wake up early for work and see our partners sleeping in?) She sets out to seek advice and validation from her family, only to find a cold reception and that she had been "replaced" by a better daughter who fulfills all of her family's requirements of what a woman should be.

Finding no answers or even solace with her family, the protagonist returns to see that her husband had made the effort to cook for her for Iftar. This story was inspired by a memory of my own partner boiling herbal soup for me (complete with whole cloves of garlic!) during the last lap of my doctoral journey. It is meant to end on a sense of homecoming in a space where one's identity and beliefs find harmony with a new set of realities.

MIND'S EYE

★★★

THE MIDNIGHT MISSION

RACHEL TEY

★ ★ ★

The face of New Year's Eve was grey and foreboding.

As thirteen-year-old Cyndy stood looking out of the window, she hoped the new year would usher in fairer skies and warmer weather. But that wasn't all she was looking forward to: when the clock struck twelve, she decided, she would begin her brand new chapter in life.

"What's on your mind, Cyn?" Drisele asked.

Just three years ago, Cyndy was an only child who occasionally fantasised about having siblings. Today, however, she lived in the company of two stepsisters, eighteen-year-old Drisele and fifteen-year-old Ana. They were pleasant enough, she supposed. Boring, but well-intentioned – sort of like vanilla ice-cream. The older girls would constantly try to involve her in conversations or invite her to things, but she seldom said *yes*. On the rare occasion she did, it was because Mama had made it an order rather than an option.

A lump came to Cyndy's throat at the thought of her mother, who single-handedly raised her after her father died when she was ten. With Papa gone, Mama became both breadwinner and head of the household. Every morning at the crack of dawn, she'd rise to prepare their meals before leaving for the cafe across the street to work as a barista. Cyndy, meanwhile, learned to be independent from a young age, travelling to and from school on her own, and ensuring the home was spick and span by the time her mother returned at the end of a double-shift.

But one day, Mama came home with news that changed both their lives. She'd met and fallen in love with one of her regular customers at the café. After marrying Tony, a wealthy widower and the father of two daughters, she and Cyndy moved into his spacious townhouse. From that point, Mama no longer worked at the café and by most counts, life got easier.

However, one thing bothered her deeply: Mama was "different" around her.

"Yoohoo …" Drisele's shrill voice disrupted her thoughts again.

Cyndy tore her gaze from the window and towards the buzz of activity in the living room. Her mother and stepsisters were decorating the house for their annual New Year's Eve party, while Tony was busy in the kitchen. She caught a whiff of his famous bread pudding and instantly felt hungry. "Sorry, I was just checking the weather. Looks like a storm's coming."

"Uh oh, I think you may be right," said Ana, joining her by the window. A clap of thunder filled the house, startling them both.

"Girls, our guests are due to arrive in less than an hour," Mama reminded all. "Cyndy, come help us put up the fairylights or lend a hand to Tony in the kitchen."

"Actually, I think I might go clean up my room?" she offered.

She'd dusted and vacuumed all day and her arms and back were still aching from the strain.

"Maybe you didn't hear me clearly the first time," her mother said slowly, the way she always did to mask her impatience. "The options were to help with the lights or in the kitchen."

Cyndy fought to suppress a surge of indignation. "But I'm tired, Mama. I was on the roster for chores today and now that I've completed them, I could really use the rest."

"Oh, it's fine, I got it!" Tony called out from behind the stove. "Dessert is done!"

"Hey Papa, I want first dibs!" Ana called back, heading for the kitchen. "Me, too!" echoed Drisele, trailing after her.

Her mother wasn't finished, however. "Everyone chips in when the family needs help," she continued, "no matter whose name is on the roster."

The mandate was clear. Help. Earn your place in this family. Always go above and beyond.

Cyndy looked at the clock on the wall. It was seven. She'd thought to activate her mission at midnight, but in her irritation she felt tempted to start five hours early.

"Dinner rolls," she blurted, as a reflex.

"Dinner rolls?" Mama repeated.

"Yes, don't we need some?" An idea was forming quickly in her mind. "Let me get them from the bakery down the road."

Her mother studied the grey clouds outside with suspicion. "I don't know if that's such a good idea. It's about to pour."

"I have my raincoat. I'll wear my boots."

"Dinner rolls, I completely forgot!" Tony cried, emerging from the kitchen to set the table. "Thanks for remembering, Cyn. Be a dear and fetch us a dozen, won't you?"

"Of course," she said, springing to action before anybody could change their minds. She grabbed her yellow raincoat off the coat stand and buttoned herself into it. "Don't worry, Mama. I'll be back shortly."

And in an instant, Cyndy was outside, the door closed behind her.

She looked up at the sky. Storm clouds hung low, threatening to unleash heavy sheets of rain. Her heart raced as she took off in quick strides.

As she walked, her mind went over the details of her escape plan. At midnight, while the countdown party was in full swing, she'd be writing a farewell note, packing up her belongings and life savings, and booking a taxi that would take her straight to Aunty Libby's. Her father's older sister, who lived in the suburbs, doted on her and would surely take her in – hopefully, legally adopt her, too.

Just as she neared her destination, a fork of lightning sprinted across the sky, accompanied by an ear-splitting rumble of thunder. Within seconds, she was engulfed in a full-fledged storm that obscured her vision and drowned out any thoughts save those of finding shelter.

Dinner rolls first, escape plan second, Cyndy decided, taking cover at the nearest bus stop. Though her raincoat and boots shielded her from the full onslaught of rain, she was still trembling from the wet and cold. If only she'd thought to bring along an umbrella for added protection.

"Buy a brolly? Only five dollars apiece."

Startled, she turned around to take in the curious sight of a gaunt and dishevelled girl. The umbrella seller, who looked to be around her age, had a dirty face and unkempt hair. She was wearing a grey dress with a green shawl draped around her shoulders and her feet were in sandals.

"I'm sorry to scare you like this," she said, with a smile that seemed to reach her eyes. "I saw you from afar and you looked like you could use an umbrella."

"Oh, it's no problem at all," Cyndy reassured her. "Did you say five dollars apiece?"

"Yes," the girl replied brightly, "and I have them in many colours and patterns." She unzipped a large tote bag she was carrying to reveal an assortment of umbrellas.

If this girl's out in stormy weather selling umbrellas on New Year's Eve, she must really need the money, Cyndy deduced. It was a shame she hadn't brought along much cash in her haste to leave the house. "I'll just take one in any design, thank you."

The umbrella seller seemed thrilled. "I have *just* the perfect one for you," she said, fishing out an umbrella from her bag. "Sky blue with seagull prints – great for beach days or thunderstorms alike."

"I'll take it!" She handed the girl a five-dollar bill and received her handsome new brolly with appreciation. "I'm Cyndy, by the way."

"Matcha," the girl replied.

"Like the drink?"

She giggled. "Actually, it's Marsha, but everybody calls me Matcha because I love green-tea-flavoured anything. Tea, cake, ice-cream, you name it."

They both laughed. Despite the urgency of the dinner rolls, Cyndy was reluctant to leave this adorable stranger. This gave her an idea.

"Listen, I'm headed to that bakery to get dinner rolls," she said. "Want to share my umbrella? They sell hot drinks there – let me buy you a cup of matcha."

The girl hesitated. "I don't know. Rainy weather is the only time I have customers."

Cyndy glanced at Matcha's tote bag, stuffed till bursting with umbrellas. "You know, my family's throwing a New Year's Eve party. Come join us, I'm sure some dinner guests could use umbrellas this rainy evening."

The girl's eyes twinkled in gratitude. "It's kind of you to invite me."

Cyndy popped open her brand new brolly and made space for Matcha to huddle under. "Come on, let's go!"

"Escape, what do you mean *escape?*" asked Matcha, taking careful sips of her hot green tea.

Dinner rolls bought and takeaway cups of matcha in hand, the girls were walking gingerly on a pavement littered with puddles. Though the storm had passed, the scent of rain lingered in the night air.

"My midnight mission is very simple," Cyndy explained. "At twelve o'clock, I leave a note, grab my things, get in a cab, and head to my Aunt Libby's."

"Wouldn't she be asleep when you arrive?" asked Matcha. "Doesn't seem very nice to wake her with your sudden arrival."

"It's perfect timing, actually," argued Cyndy, "Aunt Libby is less likely to drive me back downtown if I showed up in the middle of the night. That'll buy me some time to convince her to let me stay."

"Why do you even want to leave?"

Cyndy stopped in her tracks. "Because my mother doesn't love me anymore." She felt the sting of tears in her eyes as the words escaped her lips.

Matcha stopped too, deep in thought. "It's just that leaving home is a big decision," she said. "What makes you so sure your mother doesn't love you?"

"Well." Cyndy's voice trailed off as she called to mind the numerous instances Mama had spoken sharply to her, especially in front of Tony, Drisele and Ana. All the chores she had to help with in a much bigger house. Having to sit in on her stepsisters' inane conversations about things she didn't particularly care for. Mama's terse replies every time Cyndy mentioned their old life. Worst of all, this insistence that she focus on the present and behave like a happy, committed member of the family. Mama's smiles, hugs and cuddles had become few and far between. If that didn't signal a lack of love, what did?

The girl finished the last of her drink and exhaled in satisfaction. "This is the most delicious cup of matcha in the world," she declared.

"That's a bold claim," said Cyndy, tasting her drink and finding it far from exceptional. "It's just like any regular matcha to me."

"Oh but it's not," the girl insisted, "because I taste all your love and good intentions in this cup. In the future, every time I drink green tea, I'll remember this night we met."

They were now within metres of the house. Staring at its windows, which were draped with blinking fairylights, Cyndy thought how in a few hours she'd no longer call it home.

"Anyway I wouldn't jump to conclusions about your mother's love for you," Matcha said, steering the conversation back to the midnight mission. "If you didn't matter to her, you wouldn't have to sneak out after midnight. You could walk out in plain sight first thing tomorrow and she wouldn't even try to stop you."

Cyndy gulped. It was shocking how much sense her new friend was making. She struggled to formulate a response to refute the idea that her mother *did* love her, but the girl was already on to her next point.

"Besides, would you look at that beautiful house?" Matcha continued, gawking at the sight of it twinkling in the distance. "Not only do you live there, it's also filled with people who're waiting for you." Her voice turned wistful. "Where I come from, nobody waits for people they don't care about."

An awkward pause followed, and it hit Cyndy that she'd been so busy talking about herself she hadn't asked much about Matcha at all. Going by appearances, the girl was facing struggles of a very different kind, making hers appear almost trivial in comparison.

"Enough about me," she said, as they started walking again, "tell me more about you, Matcha."

The girl sighed. "The long and short of it is – I live with my father, but he's seldom home. So I've learned to make my own living to get by."

"When did you start selling umbrellas at the bus stop?"

"Around last year, after my grandmother died."

"It must be hard."

Matcha shrugged. "Well, when Grandma was still around she never did like the idea of me quitting school to make money." She paused for a long moment, her eyes downcast. "I really miss her, though."

"You must love her very much."

"We were close," she nodded. "I'd give anything to see her

again. Which is why I think you should only 'escape' if you're entirely sure your mother doesn't love you."

"How can I be sure?" asked Cyndy, as they arrived at her front door.

"Ask her."

She was about to protest when the door swung open. There stood her stepfather, who'd changed into an elegant suit and was looking relieved to see her.

"Thought I heard a familiar voice! And I see that we have company tonight. Hello, I'm Tony."

"Tony, this is Match – I mean, Marsha," said Cyndy, making quick introductions. "She sold me an umbrella in the storm and has no dinner plans tonight. Is it okay if she joined our party?"

"It's *more* than okay," he replied, holding the door open for the girls to enter. "Welcome to our home, Marsha."

Before the girl could respond, Drisele and Ana emerged from behind him. "You must be Cyndy's new friend. I'm Drisele."

"And I'm Ana, let us take your shawl and bag!"

"Gosh, thank you."

Cyndy chuckled at her stepsisters' eagerness. She remembered once joking that they were programmed robots, and how Mama had made her apologise.

Speaking of the lady. "You're finally home, Cyn. We were worried." Her mother came to join them, her stern expression softening to a quizzical one at the sight of Matcha. "Why, hello."

The girl looked sheepish. "My name is Marsha, and I'm sorry to impose, Mrs. –"

"Please – call me Germaine – and it's no imposition at all, my dear."

"Sorry to be late, Mama, I was held up by the rain," said Cyndy.

"I met Marsha while taking shelter at the bus stop and she sold me an umbrella."

"Then we must thank her for helping you out of a tricky situation," her mother replied, turning to the girl. "Follow me, Marsha. I'll set a place for you at the table."

"Thank you, Mrs. – I mean, Germaine," Matcha said. "Before that, maybe I could help Cyndy serve the dinner rolls to the guests?"

"Don't worry, we'll take care of that," Drisele said, as she and Ana took the bakery bags from them.

Cyndy was relieved. "Are you sure?" she whispered to her stepsisters. "I think Mama's waiting for me to start dinner."

Ana winked. "We've got you covered. Go get changed and freshen up."

Cyndy was glad that her stepsisters had held the fort while she got ready. She felt so much better after a warm shower and changing into a party dress. She had also brought her favourite red wool shawl as a gift for her new friend.

Entering the dining room, she saw that Tony had outdone himself once again with this New Year's Eve spread, which included butternut squash and carrot soup, garlic butter shrimp, roasted sweet potatoes, glazed ham, grilled artichokes, and of course, his famous bread pudding. Also gracing the table were polished silverware and flickering tea lights, although the real show-stopper was an elegant floral centrepiece. It was tradition for Mama to assemble a different bouquet every year, and each always proved more breathtaking than the previous.

The girl was easy to spot, seated in between her mother and an empty place which Cyndy presumed was hers. Although dressed simply in a room full of strangers, Matcha seemed perfectly at ease. She was close to tears when Cyndy walked up to her and draped the red shawl around her shoulders.

"What did I do to deserve such a perfect evening?" she whispered.

"Let's see …" Cyndy pretended to think. "Oh yes, you were there with an umbrella when I needed one."

"*Umbrellas*," she corrected her.

They laughed and started eating.

As dinner wore on, Cyndy found herself having a good time, but the anxiety of asking her mother the dreaded question was gnawing at her. Every time she felt like changing her mind, she'd turn to her new friend for support, and the girl would nod, as if to say, *Don't worry, I'm here.*

Finally, an opportunity presented itself midway through dessert. "You've not been yourself today," her mother was saying, as she slid a slice of bread pudding onto Cyndy's plate. "Are you all right?"

She paused, studying Mama's face. It was softened by age but still graceful.

"It's just …" she struggled, "I wanted …"

"Yes?"

A peal of laughter erupted from the other end of the table, distracting them both. Music was playing and everywhere around them, conversations were flowing freely. The longer Cyndy sat thinking, the more it seemed as if she were looking at herself from the outside in.

She needed to focus. There was information she needed from her mother. Her midnight mission depended on it. But why was she forgetting the purpose of asking?

As the words to the question evaporated from her mind, she felt an answer beginning to emerge.

"Mama," she said, "thank you for loving me."

AUTHOR'S NOTE

As you might've guessed, this short story is a loose adaptation of *Cinderella* and *The Little Match Girl*. These fairytales fascinated me as a child, but as I grew older, questions arose in my mind.

Suppose Cinderella could've found another way to empower herself without the aid of a fairy godmother or a handsome prince? I was also curious about relationships at home. In the traditional narrative, the protagonist is a victim of her toxic family. Yet we've never heard the story told from her stepmother and stepsisters' points of view. Is it at all possible they weren't the cardboard villains they were made out to be? What if — God forbid — they were actually *nice*?

The Little Match Girl is a character whose tragic fate is sealed. In the moments before her demise, she's an outsider who's forever looking in on another life that's more fortunate than her own. Things are so chaotic at home, we're told, that she's braving the harsh winter for a chance to survive. Still, I believe, there must be more to this tale about a pitiful child who only finds relief at life's end. Looking more closely, I see a brave young entrepreneur in search of the right opportunity. Her matchsticks are also fitting symbols of hope in a dark situation. If nothing else, I'll bet this character can teach us modern readers a thing or two about gratitude.

In literature or real life, I believe girls shouldn't be content to play passive heroines, or face their struggles alone. This gave me the idea to pair up the protagonists of both fairytales. So that in alternate time and place, an unlikely friendship might be the key that unlocks a mutual journey towards greater empathy, self-awareness and gratitude.

Thank you for taking this ride with me.

ONE HUNDRED FLEETING MOMENTS OF LOVE

Elaine Chiew

1.

Across two tables at the campus cafeteria, their eyes meet; she, the new lecturer, having a *tenggiri kuah kecap* and he, veteran faculty of English Lit, having *mee suah goreng*. A look enters his eyes, one she has seen enter the eyes of other men before. Cupid shooting an arrow, but he seldom shoots two at once. She registers it, is all.

2.

On a day drumming with rain, she's caught taking shelter at the campus bus-stop, skirt hem dripping. An Austin mini pulls up alongside. Driver rolls down the window. It's him. "Can I offer you a lift, Prof. Lee?" he says.

In shock, she mumbles, "It's literally two buildings away, just down the road."

Which he must've known, since it's where their offices are.

He looks through the windshield at the torrent, the road itself ribboning with rain.

"I'll get your car wet."

He says, "It doesn't matter," when clearly, it's a vintage car and it does.

She makes up her mind. Within the confines of the tidy compact space, the steaminess, the rain outside, the creaking wipers, she's reminded of *Titanic*. Laughs at her own inside joke. "What's funny?" he says. She turns, and the look must have entered her eyes then, which she never thought would happen again, but she sees he has registered it.

They exchange inanities about the rain. Her heart pounding in her ears, Komachi wisping in her fevered brain: *long, dismal rains inundating the earth…*

Awkward parting in the corridor. "Thank you for the ride, Prof. Basu."

He nods curtly. "Sorry, I don't have a towel to offer you."

3.

Outside her office, while chatting to a colleague about her latest rabbit-hole discovery on Ono no Komachi, from the corner of her eye she spies Basu retrieving a soda from the vending machine. His broad back. His eavesdropping posture.

4.

Spots him queuing at a *nasi lemak* stall. She almost calls out, but doesn't.

5.

Through the open door: standing before a whiteboard, clicker in hand, teaching. He's short, probably her height. He sees her, too.

6.

Smoking a cigarette underneath a flame tree. Wearing pilot shades. Naked want would parade across her face, so she pretends not to see him.

7.

Exiting 7-Eleven.

8.

Flyer announcement: Prof. Rajeev Basu giving a lecture on diasporic Indian literature: Kiran Desai and Rohinton Mistry.

9.

Another day, another sighting, him getting into his Austin Mini.

10.

At a departmental meet. Someone asks about his ex-wife in the hospital. A "continuing responsibility", he sighs. She mulls this over as a setback. Both avoid the cheese cubes on toothpicks, opt for the green grapes – luscious globes, almost vulgar.

11.

He walking to class, she to get coffee. He tips his head down, his turn to pretend he doesn't see her.

12.

Folded origami paper fortune-teller, numbered one to eight, but only two hidden messages: he likes me, he likes me not. Open six times like in the I-Ching. Very mixed results; only a *suaku* prospects for love like this.

13.

Lunch with colleagues. Martin and Seeraswamy discussing the new lecturer, Mary Lee – "She's strange," Martin says.

Seeraswamy sucks on a chicken thigh bone to get at all the gravy within the crevices.

"Heard she's single" is Seeraswamy's illuminating offering. "The kids all call her old maid."

"What's she teaching?" he ventures, trying not to leak interest.

Seeraswamy again, displaying no-joke, multi-tasking abilities, sucking and talking at the same time. "Eastern classics, big yawn, the kids all want to do Western Lit only what. Some more, she's researching tanka poetry by women, *wah lau*."

Martin says, "Ono no Komachi. Too long ago, dubious historical sources."

Speak of the devil, Mary Lee walks by with her tray, and as if she heard the name Komachi, her head swivels towards them. Basu receives a piercing glance. Chokes on his water.

14.

Ono no Komachi, famed Heian beauty, daughter of a lord. Legend went she tested the ardour of one suitor – Fukakusa-no-Shōshō – court noble, esteemed gentleman, by having him wait outside her door for 100 nights. He expired on the 99th!

Basu types in her name on the department network. B.A.

English Lit from University of London, M.A. Waseda University, PhD Oxford in East Asian Literature. Fluent in Japanese, Chinese and Korean.

15.

Searched her up on JStor.

16.

Tandfonline.

17.

Read all her published papers. Serious academic chops.

18.

GoogleScholar. One book: *The I-Novel in Japanese Literature Post-Meiji Restoration.*

19.

On her IG account, travel photos only – Kyoto, Tokyo, Hiroshima, three posts in the last year. Felt like an online peeping tom.

20.

Runs into her in the common area outside bathrooms. He gulps, says hello, pretends to be rushing off to class.

21.

Cafeteria: she having lunch with the department head. Nicknamed Fish-Head because of his bulgy eyes.

22.

Departmental gossip rife that she's kissing up to Fish-Head for sponsorship to the University of Hawaii at Manoa conference. Fish-Head is coincidentally newly divorced.

He feels sorry for her, he himself had his reputation shredded two years ago by the rumour mill when he divorced his wife and she was then diagnosed with cancer.

23.

Was expecting a student during office hours when she pops her head in through the door. A smile lighting up her eyes. "Prof. Basu, I bought *ondeh-ondeh* and *kuih lapis* for the whole department."

This so startles him he gives himself a paper cut.

24.

Spends tea-time hovering around the *ondeh-ondeh* to talk to her. Sial! Waylaid by Fish-Head's secretary, Mrs. Fung, who shows him the bandage on her foot – "bunion on big toe, very pain one" – and proceeds to detail her ordeal at the hospital.

25.

On her IG account, a hand-drawn portrait of Komachi with a poem. *This night of no moon/there is no way to meet him/I rise in longing/my breast pounds/a leaping flame/my heart is consumed by fire.* Oh, the insane hope this gives him.

26.

Exchanged hellos in corridor outside lecture hall.

27.

Hellos.

28.

Hellos again.

29.

Hellos turning breathless.

30.

Hellos. She's lunching with Fish-Head again, heads uncommonly close.

31.

Hellos accompanied by eye-avoidance tactics.

32.

Never knew hellos could be charged like livewire. She's checking out library books, hair up in a bun with a pencil stuck in it, her long neck. Too much, and two sightings in one day. Almost did his heart in.

33.

Caught by Martin checking her IG account. Moment of red-hot embarrassment. Martin says, "Oho, I've been doing the same, I want to go to Hawaii too."

34.

English Lit Movie Night: *Hiroshima Mon Amour*. Have a feeling she would go. Maybe this will be the night they go beyond hello.

35.

Jackpot. About to ask if the seat beside her is taken when Fish-Head swoops in and takes it.

36.

Fish-Head invites himself to a threesome after the movie. Coffee and curry puffs at Toast Box, everyone eyeballing each other. Fish-Head starts declaiming on the meaning of Hiroshima, the making of a film about it by a French director with French actors, the subtle cultural occupation subtext. As if they were undergrads in a lecture hall. Basu says the bleeding of history into bodies gave him much to think about, and the conversion of heinous barbarity – the atomic bomb – into a peace narrative was also an act of violence. She agrees, sounding very heated and intense, "The beginning of suffering for Hiroshima meant the end of suffering for the rest of the world. The peace narrative allows the whole world to forget because the locus of suffering is left in Hiroshima." Fish-Head picks his teeth with a tooth pick and says, "You forgot what the Japanese Occupation did to us?" Whenever Basu looks at her, his eyes send subtexts of their own.

37.

Couldn't say no to Fish Head about lunch. *No repeat of Toast Box please*. Basu walks past, but fortunately, only nods. Doesn't join them.

38.

Indecision: not able to go forward, not able to move back. She gives herself a pep-talk in the women's bathroom. Forty-two and behaving like a teenager. Coming out, bumps into him. "Hello,

Prof. Lee."

"Hello, Prof. Basu."

"Nice day, isn't it?"

"Yes."

Ask him! "How about coffee?"

He clears his throat, looking like she's asked to lobotomise him. Says he has a class to teach.

39.

He does have a class to teach, he isn't lying. But how could he have been struck quite so dumb? He could've countered with, *lunch tomorrow?* Watches her walking off with limp shoulders.

She turning her face up to the sky as she exits the lecture building, soaking up rays and breeze; it makes him feel crazy watching her.

40.

Mrs. Fung informs her rather importantly that someone named Hisayoshi is at reception. Her ex-boyfriend in Singapore for business. Just her luck to run into Basu at the automatic doors. Hisa with his hand on her back, possessive, and Basu's eyes round as coins. This is what happens with age. You become friends with your ex, and he asks to holiday together. A friends-with-benefits kinda holiday.

41.

She has too many suitors. Coffee with Martin.

42.

Lunch with Fish-Head.

43.

Kueh-time with Mrs. Fung.

44.

Everybody loves her. Even the students. Her office hours are packed. He retracts into his shell like a turtle.

45.

Departmental meet: Fish-Head wants to start a film club for students. #Booksthathavebeenturnedintomovies. Interdisciplinary approach incorporating film studies, literature and history. Fish-Head acting like he's the first to ever think of it. They look at each other, both roll their eyes at the same moment.

"Right! Prof. Lee and Prof. Basu shall run it together." Fish-Head claps and rubs his hands together.

46.

Afterwards, they exchange phone numbers. A moment out of time.

47.

Meeting in his office, Mary Lee looking so pretty with her hair in a bun and her flowery skirt – same as that day in the rain. They discuss how best to run the club, divide up tasks, choose an afternoon they both can make. She loves all his suggestions: *Cry, My Beloved Country, The Remains of the Day, The Godfather*. She chooses *Sense and Sensibility, To Kill A Mocking Bird*. Both hate *Forrest Gump*, both love *The Princess Bride*.

This feeling, what do you call it? Simpatico. They are simpatico. "Watching film and reading books is my idea of heaven," he says.

"Followed by an intellectual discussion afterwards. Like a post-coital cigarette," she says.

His ears burn. Mary blushes.

48.

All week, walking on clouds. He can stop her in the corridor on a million pretexts. "*Schindler's List?*"

"Oh, yes."

49.

"Prof. Lee, how many students have we got?"

"Three. And call me Mary please."

50.

"Students have asked for *Harry Potter*." She's nearly apoplectic, so cute.

"Okay, no worries, we will balance it with *Lord of the Rings*." Waggles his head, admiring his own wit. Her eyes dazzle him.

51.

"*Shawshank Redemption?*"

She's never seen it.

She agrees this needs rectifying. After her holiday.

He dares to ask who she's going with. She says, with her ex, to Borobudur.

52.

The first club-meet is frosty between them. They talk at cross-purposes, contradict each other. The students swivel their heads left to right, right to left. Anger rides just below the dialogue interface; she doesn't think she owes him any explanation. He hasn't given her a reason to.

53.

Mary Lee goes on holiday and he sees Mary Lee everywhere.

54.

At the reception automatic doors.

55.

Exhibition at the university museum on *ukiyo-e*.

56.

Bathroom common area.

57.

Staring at her office hour slots, empty of names.

58.

At the campus cafeteria.

59.

Maddeningly, whenever he sees Fish-Head.

60.

At the bus stop. Because it's raining.

61.

When he sees a woman with her hair up. Or a long neck.

62.

Can't sleep, eyebags the size of garlic bulbs. Finds a note underneath his office door. Mary has returned. "Can we meet?"

63.

Like climbing up one hundred steps, you hear the bassooning drumbeat of your own heart. She looks like she's gotten too much sun, skin boiled red. Here to discuss the next club-meet.

"Did you enjoy your holiday?"

"I did, but I went alone."

He's overjoyed that she has nobody to go with.

64.

He hasn't heard a word.

65.

A text out of the blue from Prof. Basu: "What film did we agree to screen?"

She texts back: "We didn't. It's our first screening, have to set the tone, remember we discussed this?" Puzzled emoji face.

"How about *Rashomon* or *Forty-Seven Ronin?*"

"I was thinking *Shawshank Redemption.*"

66.

Mary Lee lives in a condo unit in Clementi. He stands outside about to ring her doorbell and a sentence in her research paper comes back to him: One is conquered by a woman's face and form, yet finds inarticulable what makes her beautiful.

Because of her, he's reading Kawabata. Kawabata measured a woman's beauty by her cleanness – Mary would appreciate the hilarity of this sentiment. What most men find beautiful is not for him. The perspiration above her lip, was all it took.

67.

He brings flowers. And a bottle of wine. Stands at her threshold like he were on a date. After the film, they go to a hawker's centre. Conversation flows naturally from film to the club to teaching, from the abstract to the personal. Once he opens up, he tells her very private things. Almost eagerly. How he met his ex-wife at a college party, how marriage made him feel less of a man, the trauma of divorce, and the attendant unshirkable feelings of responsibility. Strings tied cannot be untied. Then says, "The more you wear life's scars, the more afraid you become. One becomes more emotionally fragile with age, not less." Oh, these delicious frissons of feeling passing back and forth.

68.

This morning, she goes back and forth whether to send her amateurish ink-drawing of Komachi. Would that scare him away?

Next moment, she presses the button. It whooshes off into the ether. With a heart emoji.

69.

Sees him talking to Fish-Head.

70.

Filling his titanium water bottle at the water fountain.

71.

Being waylaid by Mrs. Fung again, this time about her aquarium and the doubtful appearance of mold.

72.

No answer to her text. He was last online an hour ago.

73.

He's online now and it says…*typing*…back to online… *typing*…
then stops.

   No text.

74.

What does it mean when someone who gave you such feelings
shows up in your dream?

75.

He's lunching solo. She scrapes up her courage. Sits down across
from him. Babbling about her research, all the while this roaring
between her ears. "Prof. Basu, what did you think about my text?"

   His mouth opens in a big 'O'. He keeps stabbing at the prawns
on his plate. Then tells her Fish-Head has awarded him the
honorarium for Hawaii, although he doesn't have a paper to present.

76.

She tells herself she isn't angry, not even disappointed. But when he
pulls up at the bus stop and offers to take her home, she declines.

77.

He sees her detour to take a different route to the departmental
meet. He wants to say: You've misunderstood, I didn't even covet
it. It just happened. It was the universe's doing.

78.

During the entire meeting, she refuses to meet his gaze.

79.

"Mary, would you care to grab a coffee?"

"I have a meeting with Martin."

Love is indeed fleeting. Highly inflated.

80.

That evening, they screen *Shawshank Redemption*, and the entire 2h22m is excruciating. He keeps looking searchingly at her during the half-hour discussion time. She's engaged, lively, professional but aloof.

81.

She accepts the ride home. In the car, he blurts out, "Mary, it wasn't a stratagem. Fish-Head gave it to me because I'm a long-standing faculty member here."

"Did you tell him you don't have a paper to present?"

"No, not exactly."

"Well then, there's nothing more to be said. Enjoy Waikiki Beach."

82.

As if nothing has ever happened between them. Hellos.

83.

Smoking underneath the flame tree, he waves, she waves but keeps walking.

84.

If he stares any much more at the drawing she texted, it would bore a hole in Komachi's forehead.

85.

The drawing gives him a brainwave. Gets to work gathering what he needs for the application to the Foundation. The email reply says the decision will take a week.

86.

Longing is the blue of distance, the distance between desire and arrival. He daydreams of them at a swim-up bar drinking those cutesy drinks with pineapple chunks and paper parasols.

87.

Disco-dancing at the conference luau – he's 'Staying Alive-personified'.

88.

Sitting first-row centre as she presents her paper, clapping enthusiastically.

89.

Hiking a volcano together.

90.

Visiting a waterfall, maybe a skinny dip?

91.

Visiting the Pearl Harbour Memorial, imagining their in-depth conversation about history and collective trauma and memory.

92.

Dinner together every evening.

93.

Kissing Mary at the door to her hotel room. This daydream fragment made him stumble over the parking wheelstop, he feels so out of practice.

94.

Watches scores of YouTube videos to brush up on technique.

95.

An email notification scrolls across his phone. Tremblingly, he opens it. He got the grant.

96.

Runs pell-mell to Mary's office, sucking in his stomach so it won't look like he's jiggling a cantaloupe underneath. Hopes he won't expire on the 99th step like Shōshō.

97.

She's not in her office.

98.

Nor at the cafeteria.

99.

Mrs. Fung swats at him like a pesky fly. "I very *sibuk*, you know."

100.

Finds her outside the bathrooms. His confession sliding forth like the tide: the Foundation, the grant, the honorarium to be hers once Fish-Head is told. Now he only has to write the paper. And I love you.

They stand there grinning at each other.

Wait till he tells her his plans for Hawaii.

AUTHOR'S NOTE

Ono no Komachi, a Heian (794-1185) poetess celebrated for her waka poetry, named one of the Thirty-Six Immortals (Sanj rokkasen) was so famous for her beauty she was depicted in Edo Period ukiyo-e, and has been the subject of numerous noh and kabuki plays; Yukio Mishima wrote a short story about her, the Shinkansen to Akita is named after her, and there is even a Komachi Festival in her hometown. The legend goes that she enjoined one of her courtly suitors, Fukakusa no Shōshō, to visit her every evening for 100 days in order to win her heart, a task he set out faithfully and determinedly to do in all weathers but tragically, he perished on the 99th night.

I wanted to have some fun paralleling this Komachi legend of 100 evenings with 100 fleeting moments, each and every one based on a detail or moment I observed or collected from real life, playing with the anthology's theme of the 'real love story', but stitched into a fictitious contemporary love story with all its modern accoutrements (texting instead of poetry or letters) and resonances of Tinder swiping left and right (which also aids the point of view switches from her to him) as well as the fear of being ghosted (the modern 'rejection').

THE QUEEN OF HEAVEN

NICHOLAS YONG

It is said that on a certain day of a certain month in certain years, something unusual happens at the Grand Mazu Temple of Tainan, Taiwan.

It was a cold midwinter afternoon some years back, when I found myself wandering around the West Central District of Tainan. The area was apparently constructed via the chaos theory of urban planning, with scant emphasis on the planning part.

Take a right turn and you might find a delightfully old school store selling Japanese pornographic DVDs ('With Chinese subtitles!'). Take a left and there you are on the main street, face to face with two women sharing a scooter with their golden retriever, waiting patiently for a traffic light to turn green.

It was when I rounded a corner that I saw it: the Grand Mazu Temple, a magnificent edifice wedged between buildings old and new. Once upon a time, a tour guide might have brought me around and told me stories about it. But this is the 21st century, so I stepped over the knee-high threshold and strolled through the house of prayer with Google as my guide, the scent of incense and candles dogging my every step.

It was once a palace for the Ming Dynasty prince Zhu Shugui, before his forces were defeated by the Qing empire in 1683. Crushed by despair, the pretender to the throne is said to have told his five concubines, "Now all is lost, and the day of my death is set." And so the prince, along with the quintet of beautiful women who loved him so, hanged himself from the palace roof beams.

In 1684, the emperor Kangxi conferred the title of Queen of Heaven upon the sea goddess Mazu, and the palace was converted into a temple dedicated to her. Known by thirty-six names, Mazu oversees all living beings with the help of her guardian generals, the demons Qianliyan ("All-seeing") and Shunfeng'er ("All-hearing"). While she is the patron of sailors and coastal communities, all may call on her name. Many miracles have been attributed to her, from the ending of epidemics to the driving out of demons.

There are other gods honoured in the temple such as Yue Lao, the god of marriage and love, who is often depicted as an old man standing beneath the moon. But it is the golden visage of Mazu, resplendent in her golden royal gown and crown of nine beaded tassels, who reigns supreme as she holds the ceremonial tablet of knowledge. Above her hangs an elaborately woven banner with one of her titles: 天上圣母, or Holy Heavenly Mother.

As I stood in one of the temple courtyards and took in the ornate architecture, I was so lost in thought that I didn't even notice the old woman shuffling towards me, her open palm outstretched. Evidently, even the power of Mazu was insufficient to meet her earthly needs.

I was about to dismiss her when she asked: "Would you like to hear a story?"

I paused for a moment and took in the sight of the elderly woman. Her hair was white as snow, and her lined countenance made me think of the trails left by vehicles passing through the desert. She reminded me of Chinese period dramas from my childhood, where there were invariably elderly characters imparting pearls of wisdom.

"What is the story about?"

"It is a tale of longing and loss, of forbidden love, and Mazu's grace and mercy, which will redeem us all in Heaven's eyes."

I had to give it to the old woman: she certainly knew how to sell a pitch. So I took out my wallet and placed a note in her hand.

She grasped the money in both of her leathery hands and smiled. Then she tucked it away and cleared her throat, like a showman preparing for a performance.

"Listen carefully: I shall tell this story only once. For not all are meant to hear it, and even fewer to understand it."

On a day in the ancient past, a young man named Lin found himself at the Grand Mazu Temple. He had come to ask Mazu's blessings for a long sea journey he was about to undertake. For Lin was an only child whose parents had recently passed, leaving him nothing but the tiny house they lived in. There was nothing left for him in Tainan, and he sought his fortune in other lands.

Kneeling before the goddess with his hands clasped before his heart, Lin looked up and contemplated Mazu's solemn expression, her eyelids drooping ever so slightly. He liked coming to the temple, for he found it greatly comforting. The Lady of Luminous Grace reminded him of his own mother, who would sit him in her lap and tell him stories of the great goddess.

Once, she was human, and a Lin too: a woman of great virtue and filial piety named Lin Moniang from the city of Meizhou. His mother would sometimes tease him with the prospect that they might be kinsmen with her.

Then one day, a Taoist master named Xuantong came to her while she was still a child and gave her a book of magical knowledge. By the time she was thirteen, she had gained supernatural powers through her mastery of the tome. Some said that she saved her family from a typhoon at the age of sixteen. Others told the story of how she would stand on the shore, clothed in red, to guide fishing boats home in inclement weather. She died young, her virtue intact, and ascended into heaven as a goddess.

Bless me, Ah-Ma, Lin muttered as he genuflected the requisite three times and kowtowed another nine times. Help me to bring my parents honour, even in the afterlife. Grant me a safe journey and I shall honour you with the choicest offerings.

As he raised his head, the fragrance of frangipani filled Lin's nostrils, as if a bouquet of freshly bloomed flowers had been laid before him. The very next thing he saw when he opened his eyes was a woman beside him in a glistening blue silk tunic, offering her devotions to the Holy Heavenly Mother.

She was unlike any other woman he had ever seen before. Her smile, replete with little dimples on her cheeks, pierced into his heart. She had almond-shaped eyes that twinkled, as if she held a secret that no one else knew. Her skin was as fair as the moonlight, her full lips a shade of bright crimson. And when she averted her gaze and chastely covered her mouth with a fan, Lin knew that he had lost his heart. His gaze followed her all the way as she arose and walked away.

Who is that woman, he wondered aloud.

"She is Sister Mei," the wizened woman at the temple gate told him with a knowing smirk. "Her name has spread far and wide, for she possesses a beauty that is not of this world."

When Lin went home that night, all he could think of was Sister Mei. He had been to the temple many times and there were always female devotees, but none of them were quite as beautiful as her. Lin wondered what it would be like to have her hands entwined in his and to draw Sister Mei close to him, to hold her in his arms and gently place his lips upon hers. He was so deep in his silent reverie that he almost collided with a passerby on the street.

As Lin reached his home, he paused outside the threshold. Everything had already been arranged for his journey. He had paid half the fare, and his belongings were packed. A trusted friend had agreed to watch over the house. All Lin had to do was go to the harbour in the morning, and he would be on his way.

But Lin knew that he had to see Sister Mei again. He stepped into his house and laid down, tossing and turning for hours. When he finally drifted off to sleep, he dreamt of the beautiful woman at the temple. Sister Mei was standing beneath the moonlight in one of the temple courtyards, smiling coquettishly at him. For just an instant, he thought he saw an old man in a corner of the courtyard, shaking his head in disapproval.

The very next day, Lin went to the temple again, catching but a fleeting glimpse of Sister Mei. Over and over again, he took himself to the house of worship, with an offering here and a request to

Mazu there. But he never saw Sister Mei, who invariably stood in a corner on her own, for more than a few minutes. They did not exchange any words: she would offer him only the faintest of smiles before turning away. And yet, it felt as if their hearts were as one. He had never imagined that it was possible to feel this way about another person.

In his fervour, it never occurred to Lin to wonder why she always wore the same tunic in the same shade of blue, or why a woman of noble stature, as she clearly was, could be seen in a temple at all hours.

Lin's friends could see that all was not right. They would ask, why have you not set off on your journey? What is holding you back? But he waved off their concerns. Lin had begun to lose weight. He had not been sleeping well, and his general demeanor took on a dishevelled, slovenly look. He is bewitched, an old friend whispered. For Lin was no longer truly with them. He may as well have stepped onto that ship and sailed thousands of kilometers away.

Weeks passed, or perhaps months. Lin himself had lost track of time. But there came a moonlit evening when, at long last, Sister Mei did not merely offer him a glimpse of her. She stopped in her tracks and waited for Lin beneath the masses of red lanterns that hung from the rooftop beams. Emboldened, he strode forward.

"公子,"[1] she whispered in a voice that could melt the heart. How pale and fair she is, he thought. How lovely she is to look upon.

The air was redolent with frangipani again. Despite the candles and joss sticks burning all around them, the floral smell was as clear as day.

---

[1]   A formal term for a son of nobility.

"I am no 公子, my lady. My name is Lin." Ignoring the perplexing feelings inside of him and not caring if anyone saw, Lin

took her hands in his. As Sister Mei cast her cool focus on Lin, an understanding began to dawn upon him.

Why, he asked, are your hands so cold?

Sister Mei was as still as the idols that lined the temple. "We cannot be together."

"Why?"

"We are not of the same world."

There was a chill in Lin's heart, and it felt as if it was about to break.

"Once," she said, "I gave my life for someone I loved." After a lengthy pause, she spoke again, "My four sisters and I were concubines to a most noble prince. He was such a good man."

Sister Mei sighed. "He had a voice like thunder. But to look into his eyes was to look upon the surface of a lake, placid and still. And when the Prince took you into his arms, he was loving and gentle. It mattered not that he ultimately belonged to none of us; my sisters and I loved him with all of our hearts."

"I remember the day his forces lost the final battle with the Qing, when the Prince decided that he no longer wished to live. He urged us to leave him, telling us that we were still young and had a future. Yuan, my eldest sister, was the first to cry. But I will never forget her words. 'If the Prince lives, we all live. If the Prince dies, we all die.'"

"And so, we hanged ourselves with silken cords."

Sister Mei's eyes glittered with tears as she wept silently. "I didn't want to die. I loved the Prince, but I loved life more. But all I had in the world were the Prince and my sisters. So I accepted the cord willingly."

There was a note of bitterness in her voice now. "But they didn't bury me with my sisters. In their haste to entomb us, they forgot about me. My body was left to the Qing soldiers to defile and destroy. That is why I am still here. I have been here, all by myself, for so very long."

"So many devotees come and go in the temple, but no one ever sees me. Except you."

Lin was still. He was not afraid or troubled by what he had heard. Instead, he gently wiped her tears away, never taking his gaze off her. Sister Mei beamed at him. "You remind me of the Prince."

Lin did not say a word in return. Instead, he clutched her hands ever tighter and led her to the altar of Mazu, where they knelt before the deity. "Most Worthy and Efficacious Lady," intoned Lin. "Hear my prayer."

"All my life, I have sought to be pleasing in your sight. I know full well what is right and wrong. I have only ever sought to walk in the path of righteousness, and to reject the ways of evil."

"But now," he said with a sharp intake of breath. "There is nothing else I can do, for my heart will never be whole again.."

Lin felt like a child, inclining his head towards the impassive features of the divine lady. "I know that the human and the spirit realms are as far apart as a full-grown man is from the day he left his mother's womb. I know that in Heaven's eyes, some things can never be permitted."

The tears were welling up. "But I implore you, Ah Ma: let your divine hand be the bridge that brings us together. With all my heart, I want to be with Sister Mei." He turned towards the beautiful girl he loved with a smile. "If she will have me."

"For if we cannot be together in this world," he declared. "Then all that I wish for is to be in the next one."

But Mazu did not appear as a pure beam of light or descend from heaven on a chariot of clouds, as some have claimed. Neither did the Divine Woman's emissaries Qianliyan and Shunfeng'er materialise. Instead, there was nothing more than a hush in the great temple, as the final echoes of Lin's prayer died away. The two lovers remained on bended knee before the altar, their hands interlocked, lost in each other.

Somewhere far off, a storm was beginning. For the briefest moment, a flash of bright red robes could be seen in the thunder and the lightning.

"So, what became of them?" I asked. I must confess that I was somewhat disappointed by her tale. There were no dashing heroes, nor any demons slain. Neither was there an epic quest to be fulfilled. All it amounted to was a tragic story of a love that could never be.

"人有人道，鬼有鬼道,"[2] said the aged woman solemnly. "The natural order of things must not be disrupted, for Heaven has decreed it so."

"But Mazu is not so hard-hearted. For she is ever compassionate and merciful, and her great eye watches over all. If her favour shines upon you, anything is possible." And then in the grand tradition of storytellers everywhere, she bowed with a flourish and walked away, never to be seen again.

---

[2] A Chinese saying that means: humans and ghosts belong in different worlds.

★ ★ ★

It is said that every 10 years, on the 23rd day of the third lunar month, one can witness something unusual at the Grand Mazu Temple of Tainan, Taiwan. On that day, thousands of devotees come to celebrate the birthday of the goddess and ask for a miracle. And if you are particularly pious, and your heart yearns to please Mazu – or so the story goes – it is said that the Divine Woman will grant you a vision.

More than one person has had the vision, and not everyone agrees on what they see. Some are heartened, while others are frightened. Some are simply indifferent.

But there is a general consensus that it is a couple in what appears to be ancient clothes – she in a glistening blue tunic, he in scholarly attire – strolling side by side. He is smiling, she is covering her mouth chastely with a paper fan, and it appears as if they have all the time in the world. The couple can be seen only momentarily, before they fade away like the setting sun.

AUTHOR'S NOTE

It was in late 2018 that I stumbled upon the Grand Mazu Temple of Tainan, Taiwan, and first heard the name of the goddess Mazu And with devotees all around, amid the swirl of joss sticks and incense, I found myself thinking of that classic Tsui Hark movie: *A Chinese Ghost Story*. And once I discovered more about the history of the temple, I knew that it was a perfect setting for the tale that I wanted to tell, utilizing one of the oldest tropes in Chinese literature: a man falling in love with a ghost. Not to mention another classic trope: forbidden love.

In telling my story, I drew upon the age-old tradition of the grizzled, mysterious storyteller, while the story owes much to the influence of *The Dream Hunters* by Neil Gaiman and Yoshitaka Amano. In researching the legends of Mazu, I drew upon the writings of, among others, Jonathan Winthorpe, riley Winters, Lin Yaoyu and Lin Linchang. There is even a quote from *A Chinese Ghost Story*.

However, while my tale is almost entirely fictional, the devotion that Mazu inspires in millions across the world is not. As far as I understand, she does not typically intervene in matters of the heart. However, I like to think that she responds to virtue and sincerity with a compassionate heart. I can only hope that I have done the Holy Heavenly Mother justice.

SNOWSKIN

Jean Tay

★ ★ ★

1. BEGINNING

The rain is blinding, beating down so hard, I can barely open my eyes, let alone make out the path before me. It forces me to squint, the heavy drops beading on my lashes. The rain is turning everything translucent, leaving a pearly coating of droplets on my skin.

In this country, rain is not for the faint-hearted. While others tremble at a light drizzle, we glide fearlessly into the monsoon. Floods are nothing more than rippling ponds to us. Right.

The rain melds my hair into a single heavy rope, that weighs like a noose against my neck. The hem of my skirt trails in the mud. Then suddenly, it eases. The incessant beating, the unceasing darts.

I look up, surprised. Because the rain continues to crash down in solid silver sheets around me. And yet, I can see. Blinking through my lashes, I see a figure. Holding up a frivolously cheerful yellow umbrella. The rain slants in relentlessly, underneath the umbrella.

But at least now, I can open my eyes properly, to see the man holding up the umbrella. The one who wears an incongruously cheerful smile, looking remarkably pleased with himself, even though his shirt is completely soaked through. The rain plasters his shirt to his skin, turning the pale fabric dark. But where his skin is bare, free from fabric, it gleams in the rain, reminding me of the warmth of polished wood.

When we were young, Q and I used to pick glossy rubber seeds out of the grass. We'd rub them diligently against the pavement till they burned with heat. Then we'd chase each other around, trying to press their smooth, burning surfaces to our skins, as if we could burn a hole in our skin with the heated seeds. It was a fun but futile game. Never once did the heat of the rubber seeds penetrate our skin, no matter how hard we tried.

His fingers brush against my sleeve and I instinctively back away from him and the proffered (and practically useless) shelter. But he smiles even wider, and the umbrella tracks my retreat.

Take it. I don't need it.

And when I hesitate,

Don't worry, I won't catch a cold.

I won't either, my blood is too cold for that. But he doesn't need to know that yet, does he?

So I hold the thought in my head, and return the smile. It's nice to be the damsel in distress, after a lifetime of battle. Let somebody else play the hero in shining armor for a bit. After all, I have a soft underbelly too.

2. TOUCH

He was the first one who didn't flinch. Instead, he ran a gentle finger down the ridges of my skin, intrigued.

Has it always been like this?
Always.

I waited for the inevitable recoil. Because we were different. Because even though, regardless of race, language and religion blah blah blah … the journey always ends at a broken bridge, too far to cross.

I never meant to let him see, you know. I'm always very careful about how I cover up. It's always long sleeves and ankle-length skirts or trousers for me, regardless of the weather. So, it certainly wasn't an act of seduction. I know better than to believe that an unexpected glimpse of my lily white, almost translucent skin, would lead to any stirrings of desire from a red-blooded male. The sight was more likely to evoke an unexpected yelp, or an uncontrollable shudder, or even worse, a bully's loud blustering to cover up his cowardice. *Eeee, why you so weird one. Ewww, gross, yucks.* The responses have been pretty consistent all the way from kindergarten to primary school, through secondary school and university.

So I'm waiting, but it doesn't happen. Instead, he continues to trace the patterns on my skin, as if hypnotised.

I've never seen anything like this before. It's fascinating. Your epidermis … The level of keratinisation …

Did I mention that he was a medical student? Perhaps that helped, in dealing with the unexpected. Or perhaps in his experience of dealing with skin conditions, that's what he thought I had, a condition. His fingers are gentle, feather light.

Still, there's only so much of his scrutiny that I can take, so I jerk my arm out of his grasp. He finally looks up at me. And his eyes are as wide and disarming as always. I search them, but there's no trace of fear or irony. He breaks into a smile, crinkling the corners of those dark eyes.

What's wrong? Are you okay?

You're not freaked out?

Should I be?

I search, but there are no hidden layers of meaning in his voice.

You're different, that's all.

That is an understatement. All my life, I'd always imagined that I would be with someone more like myself. With translucent, patterned skin, and blue-veined rivers running beneath the surface. So this is new. He is literally opaque to me. I never quite know what he will say next. What he finds funny, or what triggers him, and what turns his dark eyes opaque. He tries to speak my mother tongue sometimes, but the syllables slip clumsily inside his mouth, the edges of sharp consonants rounded into smooth marbles. I can't help but laugh at the effort. And yet he tries.

It's like ... like snow.

His eyes light up, thrilled with the discovery of a new metaphor. I'm not sure if I should take it as a compliment though. He continues, hurriedly.

The tracks you find in snow. How do you say it, in your language ... Snow skin?

I begin to pull away, but he places his hand on my arm. It is warm, solid and reassuring.

His skin, as smooth as polished wood, glowing with unseen embers. His warmth slowly seeps in through the cool, scaled surface of my skin, reaching the flesh and blood within, and I finally exhale. I hadn't even realised that I was holding my breath, all this time.

For the first time, it crosses my mind. This is something I could get used to.

3. FAMILY

She spat in my face the first time she met me.

I mean, I've dealt with all kinds of rude all my life, but still.

It's not something I would have expected from the elegant woman in a Chanel suit, her hair stylishly coiffured, her make-up immaculate. But even through the flawless foundation, it was clear that the rosy hue that brightened her cheeks didn't come from rouge, but from a righteous indignation, the soul of an outraged mother, convinced that the cheap harlot before her was about to sink her fangs into her precious only son.

How dare you, she splutters. How dare someone like you ... imagine ... expect ...

Ah, if only she knew.

I think what surprises me most is the physical similarity between mother and son. They could be cast from the same mould. Certainly, carved from the same piece of wood. A fine specimen of mahogany, probably, sanded down and polished to a brilliant sheen. So that when she yells at me, lapsing into her own dialect, and spitting saliva and syllables at me, I hear him in her voice. Echoed in the way her tongue curls, the way she accents her words. And when she narrows her eyes, I recognise the same heat and fury focused in that gaze.

And with that, the differences between us are refined into a sharp blade that cleanly splits open the gap between skin and scale without spilling blood.

The best part is, she doesn't even know who I am, what I am. All this opposition stems from the fact that I am not the one she handpicked for her beloved son, particularly placed at the apex of all her connections. It's all because I had the temerity to step into the running, to present myself as a possible candidate, of his choice. She just doesn't like the fact that he made the choice, not her. That thought annoys me so much that I almost stuck out my tongue at her, but I realised that might literally give her a heart attack

To his credit, he does his best to play my defender. Boldly thrusting his body between ours, as if to block the vitriol spurting from her lips. It's like watching a dormouse battle a lion. There is no way he can fight that gorgon of a mother. She has had years of experience battling with her own in-laws, has accumulated too many insults and curses in her arsenal. She is not above destroying her own beloved son to get what she wants. And that, that is what I cannot take.

So, I smile as sweetly as I can, and slide my arm into his, and mouth, *Let's go*.

And that frightened mouse of a man does the bravest thing I have ever seen him do. He turns around, and starts to walk away from the woman who gave him life. I can feel his arm tremble, just slightly against mine, but otherwise, his back is ramrod straight, as tall and proud as any mahogany. And I am pleased to note that the insults, when flung into our backs, feel like nothing more than pesky raindrops bouncing off my skin.

As we leave, I turn back and flick my tongue out at her. Her eyes widen, she blinks, trying to make sense of what she sees. And for the first time that day, her mouth gapes open without sound.

We walk out into the sunlight, in triumphant silence.

4. WEDDING

It wasn't conventional, by any means. If you were romantic, you could say we eloped. But really, we just found a small quiet hotel room, and an obliging Justice of Peace, and prayed to whatever powers that be, that his mother wouldn't find out about it.

But by then, he had already moved out the family home for almost a decade. She periodically tried to persuade him to move home, through whatever means she could – blackmail, bribery, threats, and other assorted relatives. But he resolutely blocked her calls and stood up to her, for the first time in his life.

Being with me helped to give him a spine, he claimed. I replied that it wasn't difficult, one just had to find something that one believed was worth fighting for. He wound his fingers around the loose coils of my hair, and smiled that he had. I rolled my eyes at him.

That was the first time he asked me to marry him. I told him he was a fool and whacked his head to make sure he knew it. That didn't stop him from asking though, every year, at the most inconvenient of places.

Q never approved of the whole thing, but still, she found it rather amusing.

Oh, he's got that look in his eyes again. I bet he's got the ring in his pocket, Q would nudge me.

As long as it's not his mother's, I retort. *As if I would allow myself to be bound to a mere man. And lose everything else that I have, everything that I am.*

But Q looks at me. Because she knows. Even though she doesn't approve. She knows me better than myself.

And what is it that you're so afraid of losing?

The answer to that question kept changing over the years. And the better I got to know him, the smaller and smaller that answer became. Until there was hardly any point in keeping score any more.

I might as well say yes, I tell Q, even though she didn't ask.

You might as well.

She shrugs. A pause, and then.

I don't have to be your bridesmaid, do I?

You know I don't do that kind of shit, I reply.

And she smiles. But yes, she's still the one who stood guard outside the dingy hotel room that February afternoon, holding my bouquet for me, and calling us a cab, so that we could drive off into the sunset towards our happily ever after.

5. BREAKING

We never get there.

And after all that we've been through, after everything that we've overcome, it's the simple things that break us. Not the epic conflicts that crush us, but the mundane, everyday frictions that wear us down. The differences that made one so fascinating, so refreshing to the other, now require painstaking effort and bridge-building to overcome. And when we stopped trying, we left a trail of broken bridges and misunderstandings between us.

We have arguments, small ones, misconstrued words, miscommunication. Little cold wars that never really erupt into full-blown fights. He tends to avoid conflict, and I... it's just not in my nature to get hot and bothered about anything. Cold and bothered, that's something else altogether. My eye-rolling and audible sighs are meant to be heard, meant to trigger some kind of response. So when he doesn't respond, then does that mean he doesn't really care? His opacity, so intriguing and refreshing at first, becomes a source of frustration.

Aren't you going to say something?

What can I say?

And his shoulders slump. I think it's that action, more than anything, that gets to me. That act of defeat, without even putting up a fight.

So I tell myself that I don't need someone like him to take care of me. It's my own fault that I got used to him. And if I'm so used to him, does that mean that in his absence, he would become someone I actually "need"? I shudder at the thought. When did I become so weak?

I need my space. I disappear to Q's for a couple of days. And yet, he freaks out when I am not home, and he can't reach me. He spends hours searching in the park, he second guesses everything that we've done. By the time I return, he is furious.

Where have you been?

At Q's.

Again? What for?

I just needed some space.

Space? From me?

Stop asking so many questions. It's not always about you.

Why didn't you answer the phone?

You know I don't like answering the phone.

So how in the world am I supposed to know what is going on? Something could have happened to you. You could have gotten hurt.

I can take care of myself.

Of course. But I'm supposed to take care of you now. I'm your husband. You're my wife.

He says that with an air of authority, as though I am his property, branded with his seal.

Stop saying that. I'm not part of your property, I don't belong to you.

I didn't mean it that way.

Do you want to put me on a leash now?

Of course not.

As though I was a pet, or a performing animal? Do you want me to start jumping through hoops? Or rise out of my basket when you play your flute?

Don't talk nonsense. I just want to know what you're going through.

And I just need my own space.

Why can't you let me in?

Because a woman needs her own space, to hold her own secrets. Because there are some things about me that I'm afraid even you can't deal with.

I didn't say it aloud, but there it was. Even after all those years, what I feared most, was his fear of me. I was afraid I didn't deserve his unconditional love.

That, and the fact that he could never really sever his ties with his mother. How could he, when she was the root from which he stemmed? Years later, they still shared the same complex, convoluted root system. And yes, she turned up again, five years after our marriage, when his father got sick and she insisted he attend to the old man and spend long hours at his deathbed.

So, in the end, it isn't a single breaking point. It is a multitude of hairline fractures, a cobweb of cracks. Taken together, the membrane that binds us together cannot hold, the skin tears open, and we fall through the gaps.

I pack my bags and move to Q's. There's space for me there, there always is.

6. CHILD

It turned out to be more than a figment of my imagination. Or a spoilt curry that caused my stomach to churn.

It didn't even hit me when I was bent over the toilet bowl,

regurgitating my breakfast for the third time that week.

It was Q who put the unspoken thought into words, when I complained to her that the milk must be off.

Impossible, I said.

That's what I said when you two got together, and look what happened.

I swallowed my retort and headed down to the pharmacy for a pregnancy test. But it was really more of a formality to confirm what we both already knew.

In the end, the stirrings of new life turned out to be less like butterflies beating their wings, and more like larvae squirming in my belly. Still, it kept me company at night in my borrowed bed, when I found myself missing the pull of his fingers through my hair, combing out my knots.

I spent hours wondering if it would inherit the iridescence and pattern of my skin or the rich colour and clarity of his. Whether I would see my pale, almond eyes reflected there, or his large ebony ones. And then, inevitably, I would start thinking about those familiar dark eyes and how the skin around them crinkled when he smiled. Ridiculous.

Aren't you going to call him? asks Q.

For what? I retort.

She shrugs. She knows, better than I, what I'm going through. But she also knows better than to push.

In the meantime, my belly swells, ripens, pushes my skin taut, until there is no longer any question of the impending arrival. Still, I try to behave as I always have, buying groceries, running errands, jogging around the estate on my own. It's on one of these supermarket runs that I encounter her. It's been years since I've seen her. I've managed to avoid all those awkward family dinners. She hasn't aged well at all, but I recognise her at once. Her eyes widen slightly as she registers my swollen belly, behind the shopping trolley. I nod with as much composure as I can muster and then push off on my way again. She calls out my name, but I choose to ignore it, concentrating on keeping my spine ramrod straight.

I suppose it's no coincidence that he shows up the very next day, at Q's doorstep. That unreliable, double-dealing sister of mine lets him in without a fight, smirking as if to say, *I told you so.*

By the end of the week, I find myself packing my bags again. As Q helps me load my luggage into his car, she whispers, *this is what you need and you know it.* I stare daggers at her.

He is an angel. Massaging my heavy feet, singing songs to my swollen stomach, driving out at midnight to satisfy my cravings. He does everything he can to melt the ice between us. He makes himself indispensable again, and fool that I am, I allow him. I tell myself that it's for the sake of the child.

Q is the one who prepares me for birth, rolling up her sleeves in her usual no-nonsense way. I know I'm in her safe hands, but I don't want him to be present for the birth. I'm not sure he can take it, seeing me in that state. All my fears and worries come crashing back in full force. But he insists, and Q herself doesn't think it's a big deal.

An extra pair of hands will come in handy, she says.

But what if …

If he goes, he goes. And if he stays, he stays. Since when were you so scared?

In any case, he takes it for granted that he will be there, no questions at all. I'm too tired and bloated to fight with him. And honestly, when I'm screaming bloody murder as the contractions kick in, it's good to have his hand to hold on to, again.

So, he sees it all, my unnatural contortions, my loss of self-control. He sees me exactly as I am. The pain of labour lays everything bare. And yet. He's still there. Paler than I'd ever seen him.

And yet. He's still looking at me in the same way as he did before. Without fear, without judgment. He smiles as he gazes down at our pale-skinned child in the cot.

He's beautiful, he says. *Just like you.*

As I stare into the child's dark brown eyes, I feel that jolt of recognition. I cannot deny the bloodline that runs through him. That this child, who has inherited my skin and his eyes, is the transcendent product of two long and complex lineages.

And that is why I bite my tongue, when the woman turns up at our apartment four weeks later.

Also, she carries a pot of soup in one hand, and a bag of diapers in the other. Poor weapons for battle, if you ask me.

Of course, I had been dreaming of my revenge for years, of how I would hiss spectacularly at her in our ultimate showdown ... Except that this wasn't the woman I remembered. Up close, I can see that the loss of her husband and the long years of caregiving have taken their toll on her. Instead, an elderly woman with mottled skin and crow's feet stands before me, grey hair escaping from a loose bun.

Who's there?

He calls from the bedroom where he is changing the baby's diapers.

Come and see.

In the meantime, she awkwardly offers up the tribute she has brought, two packs of diapers, a carton of bird's nest and a large thermos flask of some home-brewed soup. She might as well have come bearing a white flag.

He takes a few more minutes to emerge, carrying the freshly changed baby. And does a double-take when he sees his mother.

What are you doing here?

But she completely ignores him. Her attention is entirely focused on the child nestled in his arms.

Can I? she says.

I hesitate at first, but as far as I can see, there's no hidden meaning behind her words, or in her outstretched arms. To his credit, he looks at me first, and it's only when I nod that he finally passes her the child. She gathers the child to herself, caresses his translucent skin and coos over his dark brown eyes. His pale skin contrasts sharply against her dark one, but she doesn't seem to notice.

Contrary to popular belief, I'm not one to carry hate within me for centuries. My heart is a lot warmer than people give me credit for.

7. ENDING

This is the part of the story that is never told. It takes place after eight years of ordinary moments, both mundane and transcendent.

By now, the woman's head of brilliant white hair is stark against her dark brown skin. The skin is no longer smooth and polished, but gnarled and wizened like tree bark. Her once-ebony eyes are clouded with cataract, almost as pale as mine. The woman, with a feeding tube in her nose, who can no longer spit and curse, but gurgles and hums lullabies from her youth. She is far more beautiful now than she ever was in her prime.

He does whatever he can. Which honestly isn't much. Because for things like this, you need a female touch, it's as simple as that.

And she needs me. After all these years, I am no longer foreign to her. She holds my pale hand between hers. She always calls for me, my elegant name transformed into simple syllables that she can hold in her mouth.

I wash what's left of her silky white hair with my own hands, and carefully wind its loose tendrils into a bun at the nape of her neck. I blend boiled carrots and cauliflower into a fine paste, which I mix with broth and pour down her feeding tube. And for a special treat, I sometimes mash ripe mangoes and let the taste sit on her tongue.

The child brings her much joy. Her arms are always open to him, bearing more love and tenderness that she'd ever shown to her own flesh and blood. Through the three of them, I've learnt more about the nature of love and desire and dependency than I imagined possible. I've allowed myself to need and to be needed. Somehow, I have been entwined in this family, I've made my home within their branches, my blood flows in their veins now.

We sit together in the park, three generations of one family. She and I, sitting at the bench, watching the boy and his father on the stone bridge, as they throw bread to the fish in the lake. The surface of the lake starts to ripple, a light drizzle, barely there. But just in case, I pull open the umbrella from my bag, and hold it over her head. She turns to me, placing her veined hand on my ridged arm.

Together, we watch our boys, one mahogany-brown, the other snow-skinned, dance in the rain.

AUTHOR'S NOTE

Since young, I have been fascinated with the story of Madam White Snake, and the duality of this beautiful woman who trod the fine line between powerful snake demoness and misunderstood heroine and wife. On one hand, here was an immensely powerful heroine with superhuman abilities, who was busy fighting epic battles against powerful villains, with her sister, Green Snake (also known as Xiao Qing) by her side. But on the other hand, there was her strong desire to settle down with an exceedingly ordinary and weak human being, and set up a family with him. And it was sometimes hard to imagine how those two worlds fit together.

As the years rolled on, I realised that some of our most heartbreaking ordeals and heroic acts actually lie much closer to home than we expect. They take place every day, quietly behind the closed doors, where even the simplest acts of kindness can contain divine notes of grace. And so, I found myself writing, not an epic myth, but a normal, everyday story, one of ordinary people dealing with life and relationships and their extraordinary capacity to adapt, to forgive and to love.

MODERN

LOVE

* * *

MY GIRL IN SINGAPORE

VICKY CHONG

19 DECEMBER 1998, SAN JOSE, CALIFORNIA, USA

A message popped up as soon as Brian entered the ICQ.

Hello:)

Hi! Brian from San Jose. New to ICQ. I just installed my brand new PC, which I had bought myself for my fiftieth birthday.

He didn't know what made him reply or enter the chat room. Outside of his job, he had never taken any intiative to connect with any stranger before.

Pearl from Singapore. New to ICQ too. When was your birthday?

7 December.

Happy Birthday, Brian!

Thank you! What time is it in Singapore?

10pm. I've just had my dinner.

She sent a photo of her dinner. Plates of stir-fry and a bowl of broth.

Looks delicious. It's 7am here. I'm having my cup of coffee.

Brian flipped open the atlas on the shelf and found Singapore, a speck at the tip of Malaysia. South of Vietnam. He had been a soldier in the Vietnam War at twenty. He remembered the time he spent in Asia. Except for the war, he liked everything about Asia, especially the petite women with their gentle, caring ways.

The droning of Brian's PC broke the silence of the house, quiet in this early hour and would remain mostly so throughout the day and night as the wife and son went about their lives. Left to his own devices, Brian rarely heard his own spoken voice at home, but here in the ICQ, he was noisily chatting with this thirty-three-year-old Chinese woman as if she was sitting right across from him, sharing a cup of coffee.

This became Brian's morning routine. Coffee, ICQ, Pearl in Singapore. This felt safe. She was far away.

4 JUNE 2003, MODESTO, CALIFORNIA, USA

"Hey, buddy, over here!" Brian waved to Lou as he entered the bar. Lou swaggered purposefully across, like the uniformed cop he once was on an investigation. Soon, they were smoking between shots of whiskey and exchanging stories. Lou had served in the Vietnam War too.

Brian told Lou about Pearl. "Her innocence, I find it attractive. I can't explain the connection between us. We've been video chatting on Yahoo every day for the past two years. Her three children sang me Happy Birthday on my birthday, like I have another family in Singapore."

An image of Pearl and her children appeared and Brian realised how much he missed them while sitting here in the bar. "You know, there are times I wished Pearl had come into my life earlier.

This is so unlike me, one who is diagnosed with an emotional detachment disorder (EDD)."

Brian couldn't help thinking how near he was to her, when he was stationed in 'Nam, except she would have been a four-year-old. Or that in '88 when Pearl was on a holiday in San Francisco. Maybe they passed each other in front of the Golden Gate Bridge? His office was near there.

Lou leaned in. "Look, 'Nam affected many of us and we're still coping in our own small ways. So, you met this divorced woman online whom you like and want to move to Singapore to be with?" He paused, as if pondering deeply on a clueless crime case. Then a grin. "What's stopping you? You're separated, kids are gone, there's nothing holding you back. Just treat it as an adventure. Don't like it, come back. The point is, you're taking the next step to healing yourself."

Lou just gave Brian the endorsement he needed.

Pearl was more apprehensive when Brian told her the plan. "A one-way ticket? You've terminated your lease of your apartment and sold your truck? Are you certain about this?"

"$7000 for the truck, it's all the cash I have. I really want to do this. Do you want me there?"

"Don't regret if I don't live up to your expectation as your girlfriend, the sexy Asian woman American men imagine. I am short and I need to lose weight."

"I know exactly how you look. Pearl, honey, sexy is not a body. Sexy is an attitude. You're smart, confident, and talented in so many ways. Just the way you built up your own PC awed me. I really want to do this. Do you want me there?"

Pearl smiled, her round face lit up like a grinning sun in an illustration in a children's book.

1 AUGUST 2003, SINGAPORE CHANGI AIRPORT

While waiting for his luggage at the arrival hall, Brian searched the crowd on the other side of the glass screen. Tired from the long flight, he was excited about his adventure but anxious too. *What if Pearl decided not to turn up? What then?* But then he spotted her. She waved, jumping up and down. Brian straightened his blazer. He had dressed up carefully for their first meeting, and he hoped she noticed.

Despite the tender hug at the airport, the conversation in the taxi to Pearl's house was awkward. Pearl pointed out the places of interest and stole glances at Brian, smiling shyly when their eyes met. To put her at ease, Brian took her hand resting between them and squeezed it. Another initiative towards his healing process, he thought. She tightened the grasp and the tension slipped away. They were once again on familiar turf.

28 JANUARY 2004, SINGAPORE

All eyes were on Brian, the only Caucasian, as soon as Pearl, the children and he arrived at the restaurant for his first Chinese New Year reunion dinner.

Pearl's three eldest brothers and their family were already seated. Other than one brother who had visited earlier to check Brian out, Brian was meeting the extended family for the first time. Pearl's mother, whom the children addressed as Ah Mah, greeted the children warmly, but as soon as she saw Pearl and Brian, her lip pursed. She had disapproved of their relationship and moved out of Pearl's house just before Brian moved in. They were only allowed to attend this dinner because Ah Mah had missed the children and wanted their presence.

Brian stepped forward to hand Ah Mah a gift box when

Pearl introduced him. Ah Mah's eyes widened as she opened the box and saw the wooden birdhouse he had carved and painted, with a Chinese red roof with twin golden lanterns hanging at two corners. Pearl decorated the orange walls with the Chinese characters associated with Chinese New Year — Spring and Fortune. Everyone crowded around to admire the gift.

Ah Mah's face remained aloof, but she nodded her thanks.

1 AUGUST 2008, SINGAPORE

The rejection letter for Brian's PR application arrived. Despite living in Singapore for five years and holding a position as Head of English Department (HOD) in a private school, at 60, he was deemed too old to be of any value to Singapore, according to Pearl. Brian shrugged. He wasn't too overly concerned, and neither was Pearl. Life was perfect as it was.

30 APRIL 2012, PHNOM PENH, CAMBODIA

Pearl's sunny face appeared on video.

"I missed you," said Brian.

"I missed you too. The house feels odd without you." She swung the camera to her mother, who waved. "Ah Mah asked if you're eating well there."

"Tell her not to worry. There's a restaurant nearby owned by an American man which serves excellent food. But I miss her *yong tau foo*."

Pearl chuckled. "Remember how angry she was when you first moved in with me? She didn't speak to me for six months."

"She couldn't resist my charm. Who knew courting my girl would include courting her mother too."

Pearl rolled her eyes. "Not your charm but your offer to paint her flat lah. She said you did such a fabulous job, she rented out her apartment at a good rate."

"Did she really say that? You've never told me." Brian was pleased to hear this, even if it was belated.

"She still looks longingly at the Chinese birdhouse every time she walks past it. The gift which thawed her heart." Pearl giggled. She said something to Ah Mah and they laughed at the memory.

"We're now back to talking on video chats like we used to when I was in the US."

"You should have applied for PR again, like I told you to when you were still employed as HOD in the school, to show your sincerity. Or at least hold on to that job to remain in Singapore. You enjoyed teaching."

"Pearl, honey, we've been through this many times. They rejected my PR application once. They will not give PR to a man who's past his prime, even if he's employed. I am sixty-four. Besides, I want to draw on my US pension."

"But now you're alone there ..." said Pearl, her voice, thick with sadness, choked.

"You know the plan, Pearl. Stay for three weeks, Singapore for a month. I'll be with you more than in Phnom Penh." Brian's voice was more cheerful than he felt. Budget air had arrived at the right time. He was prepared to clock frequent miles on Tiger Air and Jetstar every two months to visit his girl in Singapore.

Brian knew what Pearl was thinking at the moment, even if she didn't voice it out. She had that pensive look, bordering on regret. They could have gotten married during the decade they were together in Singapore. That would have been nice if both were not already put off by marriage after their divorces. Plus Pearl didn't want to mess up her financial situation by remarrying. The beneficiaries for her HDB flat and CPF were accounted for. Her mother and children were her first priorities, Brian respected that. Also, she had mentioned that she was the first in the extended family to have broken the pristine tradition by getting a divorce. To remarry would invite gossip and worse, to remarry an *ang moh* would be awkward for her mother in front of the relatives.

"I miss holding your hand in bed when I sleep," Brian said. 'But otherwise, I am fine."

"I can't wait for us to be together in two weeks. Ah Mah is looking forward to her first trip to Cambodia. I am so happy she has this opportunity to travel. If not for you, she might not want to go."

Brian was also looking forward to showing them around Phnom Penh and the tour of Angkor Wat.

10 SEPTEMBER 2016, JOHOR BAHRU, MALAYSIA/ SINGAPORE

Pearl's face was drawn when she picked Brian up from his JB apartment to drive across to Singapore. Ah Mah was in ill health and the prognosis was not good. Since Pearl's retirement seven months before, she had suggested Brian move to JB so he could travel back and forth between both countries on a tourist pass. She could also visit him more often. His brand-new three-bedroom apartment in JB was a ten-minute drive from the Causeway.

They breezed through both JB and Singapore immigration. Brian's heart skipped a beat when he flipped open his passport.

"Pearl, I am only allowed to stay seven days in Singapore this time."

"But the tourist pass is for a month."

"Not anymore. For me, anyway."

The worry of not being able to stay longer in Singapore weighed heavily on Brian's mind, as he wanted to be near Pearl in case Ah Mah's condition deteriorated. That night, his mind was not on the Korean drama streaming on the PC which he and Pearl had been watching. Her eyes might be staring at the screen, but he could tell she was worried, either about her mother or him. He hated to be another cause of worry for her during this difficult period.

"Perhaps it's time we get married," Brian blurted, surprising himself.

Pearl shrugged nonchalantly. She didn't appear surprised or happy at the proposal. He wondered who was the one with EDD now.

Brian wasn't sure if getting married was what she wanted, but somewhere deep inside, he did not want to delay this any further. Being separated from her at this lowest point proved too unbearable. How could he risk not being around for her in the event of Ah Mah's demise because of immigration issues?

Brian tried again, just in case she didn't hear him right the first time. "Do you want to get married?"

Without meeting his gaze, Pearl tried to conceal her smile. "Do you?"

Brian suddenly realised he was doing this all wrong. Just a few months before, Pearl's daughter had received an elaborate proposal from her boyfriend in full public view, with balloons and flowers. He couldn't match that, but his girl deserved a better proposal than what he had just done.

9 OCTOBER 2016, SINGAPORE

Ah Mah passed away peacefully this morning, surrounded by the family. Brian was glad he listened to Pearl and arrived in time to bid her farewell. He and Ah Mah shared an affection for each other which surmounted language and cultural differences. She was as dear to him as a mother.

When Pearl called yesterday, urging him to come to Singapore quickly, he had been hesitant.

"Ma won't last long. You have to come to say goodbye," Pearl said.

"I get only seven days in Singapore and wouldn't be able to enter again until two weeks later. I don't want to risk not being able to go when you really need me."

"You need to see her one last time."

"Let's be rational. I would rather be there to support you when Ah Mah passes on. As it is, we don't know when this would be."

"Just come, Brian."

Brian's seven-day visitor pass was just sufficient for him to participate in the five-day Buddhist wake and funeral as Ah Mah's future son-in-law.

6 NOVEMBER 2016, SINGAPORE

Dressed up in his best formal wear, Brian led Pearl to the living room where her now-adult children were seated on the sofa. They were quiet but there was an air of excitement as they looked on expectantly, the same way they had glanced upon the night sky when they were little kids, waiting for the fireworks to start during the annual National Day Parade.

Brian took Pearl's hand, went down on one knee, presented her with a bouquet and a ring, and asked Pearl to marry him. She grinned cheekily and looked around the room, as if unsure. Pearl's children yelled *YES!* and Brian wasted no time slipping the ring on her finger.

According to Chinese tradition, as a mourning couple, Pearl and Brian needed to be married within one hundred days or they would have to wait three years to wed. They immediately planned to hold their wedding on Brian's 68th birthday next month.

13 NOVEMBER 2016, CAUSEWAY

"Would you be returning to JB again?" the officer at the JB immigration booth asked, waving Brian's US passport.

"Is there a problem?" said Pearl.

"He has exceeded the maximum number of days allowed in the country. He cannot return."

Shocked. They had not expected this. A heavy gloom, ballooning every second, filled the car during the brief drive across the Causeway to Singapore.

At the Singapore immigration, the officer returned Brian's passport and when he flipped it open to check, he might have groaned aloud without intending to or else Pearl sensed his draining emotion.

"What now?" asked Pearl as she drove, trying to keep her eyes on the heavy traffic in front as they exited immigration.

"I am allowed only three days in Singapore."

"Not seven days?"

"Not anymore."

"And you can't return to JB?"

"That's the situation."

"So within three days, we need to figure out how you can remain in Singapore?" Pearl's statement came out as a question which was on both their minds.

Although Brian had spent thirteen years in Singapore, his future with Pearl was now in crisis. He couldn't bear the thought of leaving Pearl and the family and moving to Cambodia again. Singapore had become his home. He had gotten familiar with the heartland neighbourhood. There was a regular spot downstairs at the void deck where he had his smoke. The folks at the market and *kopitiam* saw him often, either slurping *yong tau foo* or eating *briyani*. The provision shop uncle looked forward to him popping in for his weekly cigarette purchase. He was the only Caucasian mingling amongst the locals in the Residents' Committee (RC) where Pearl volunteered. At the opening of the newly renovated RC office, Brian represented one of the other races in Singapore, and stood next to the MP and a few other ethnic representatives as they cut the ribbon during the opening ceremony.

Brian was retired, with no economic value to Singapore. Their marriage would not result in any contribution to the population like other younger couples. A long-term pass for a foreign spouse seemed impossible, but this was their remaining hope for Brian to stay in Singapore.

14 NOVEMBER 2016, SINGAPORE IMMIGRATION DEPARTMENT

Brian looked at the pair of women, one of whom was his fiancée, who was sobbing as she spoke. The kind female officer listened, one comforting arm around Pearl as she explained why they needed an extension for Brian. Her mother had just passed away and their wedding day was scheduled next month, within the one hundred days as stipulated by Chinese customs. To prove they were not having a fake marriage, Pearl brought along photo albums. There were photos of her children from the time they were in primary school until university graduation. Brian appeared in many of them.

"This is you?" asked the officer, turning to him and pointing to the heavy-set man he once was in a photo.

"113kg when I first arrived, to 79kg now," Brian said, with a hint of pride. "I am the weight I was when I was a high school senior swimmer," he added, albeit unnecessarily, but she was impressed.

An extension of forty-five days was granted.

7 DECEMBER 2016, SINGAPORE

A double happiness today. Brian turned sixty-eight and married Pearl eighteen years after they first met online. Their wedding was solemnised by a Justice of Peace at home, in front of Pearl's children and close friends, followed by a Chinese wedding banquet lunch at a restaurant. The bride was beautiful in a stylish white pants suit. Brian's spirit soared as he looked at his new wife, who had managed to make him attach himself emotionally to her.

7 DECEMBER 2020, SINGAPORE

Pearl and Brian will celebrate their fourth wedding anniversary on his 72nd birthday. He has been renewing his one-year long term visit pass annually since.

AUTHOR'S NOTE

When I first learnt from Pearl, a childhood friend, that she had been chatting with an American man online, I had cautioned her against conmen who preyed on vulnerable divorced women. When Brian flew to Singapore on a one-way ticket twenty years ago, I admit I was sceptical about his intentions.

A tale about an autumn romance might lack the wild passion but Brian's love for Pearl fascinated me. He had been living in a mostly white environment in California and coming to Singapore was a cultural shock — the weather, the food, to living with Pearl's mother and children in a HDB flat. So well-adjusted is he now that he is a Korean drama addict, like Pearl.

In my interview with Brian for this story, he could not pinpoint the reason he gave up his life in the USA to come over, except that he wanted to be with Pearl. He had rarely initiated any major action before, having gone with the flow his entire life, thus this was out of character. Ironically, to remain close to Pearl, he had to move to Cambodia and Malaysia because they had not foreseen the immigration problems which had made their lives together their biggest challenge.

MARRIED PEOPLE

Noelle Q. de Jesus
★ ★ ★

Connie could never tell when it might arrive, triggered by Sid's words, Sid's actions, the very reality of Sid. Rage rose from her gut, careening through her body trying to find an exit like it was projectile vomit threatening to choke her. Rage made her gasp. It made her shake and seethe. That word, seethe, was one she recalled reading in stories. But only now did she understand what it meant.

That she never knew it was coming was the worst thing; it was always out of nowhere. On an ordinary day, while she sliced up fresh fruit for their breakfast, Sid would be there, making the coffee, because the coffee was his thing. And then he'd say something.

The words struck her down … like a virus, instantly infectious, while (it did occur to her) she brandished a very sharp knife for the fresh melon or grapefruit or mango she sliced. Whatever he said instantly took the sweetness out of the fruit, sucked out its juice, its very flavour. Or it might happen as they sat on the sofa, with the dinner she made still tight and warm in their tummies. Or while they walked the dog, an ageing, malodorous, Labrador bitch, he made a remark, almost without thought, off the top of his head.

Rage made her weak in her limbs and joints. She had no recourse, as her son would say, but to "go ballistic". The argument started out with a false calm, and then rapidly escalated, until all at once, Connie lost control, fell out of her depth, buckled down to hopelessness. She was taken down, low and lost in wild woods so dense and deep and dark, she could not see it for the trees.

It might be about black people. Or the second amendment. It might be about feminism or homosexuality or bisexuality, or just sexuality in general. It might involve the rights of women over their bodies. Or about what the President said or did or did not do or did not say. And it wouldn't even be anything all that objectionable, to begin with. But its implications. Just a phrase … or sometimes, just a pause or a tone. The way he said it. Incensed, Connie picked and picked and picked at it, like it was an insect bite, till Sid too, lost it, turning sarcastic, cruel and mocking. And all at once, it was late, late at night, and they settled to sleep in stony silence. Only Connie couldn't sleep.

Many nights, she placed her pillow across her face, wishing she had done it earlier, wishing she had not said the regrettable, and sometimes, even wishing she possessed the strength to press down harder so she might stop breathing and halt the rage altogether. Sleep was a sweet escape. On too many days of such terrible discord that were no longer worth words, she forced herself to be silent, to say nothing, like she was grasping her throat in her own hands. She headed downstairs for a glass of orange juice. She'd splash an inch or so of vodka into that. And then, afterwards, lying next to

Sid, relaxed and warm, sleep would come for her, seductive, loving and compassionate. As she drifted off, Connie wondered when it was exactly that Sid had changed so, how had it happened that overnight, he had turned into someone she did not even know. The only thought that remained, days and weeks after the rage finally seeped out of her body, was this. Maybe, she had never really known him at all.

Connie did not remember what she was wearing the day that they met, but Sid did. He remembered it well, and the memory, when he opted to indulge in it, was a pleasant one.

They met on her first day on the job as a junior visualiser for the in-house ad shop of a personal products company. This was back in the time when people still used paper and coloured wax crayons to design and illustrate campaign concepts and collateral. Something had touched him about her navy blue pencil skirt, half an inch or so too long, and the pale, sleeveless halter blouse in floral print tucked snugly into it. She wore her hair long and loose back then, left it in unruly curls down her back, so on that first day, they covered her bare shoulders.

Her boss had asked her to sit in at a meeting to discuss new product packaging, and after introductions, they all sat down. Sid made eye contact with her and then used her name for the very first time, enjoying it on his lips.

"Connie, do you use Easy Panty Pads?"

Taken aback, Connie answered, "Excuse me?"

She tried to remember his name. "Sid?"

He liked that, too.

Sid held up the cardboard packaging.

"Easy Panty Pads. Do you use them? And if so, how do you like them?"

The account executive passed Sid over with a narrowed glance and a sigh but said nothing. She had worked with him for years and knew his ways. Connie felt hot and embarrassed in her cheeks and ears, though there was certainly no earthly reason why he should not have asked her this question, even so pointedly. Later on, over lunch, he confessed he asked everyone that. He had handled the account for two years; it bothered him that this was the only product of which he had no intimacy or direct knowledge.

It would be months before it occurred to Connie that Sid might be attracted to her. One would think, Connie mused, that someone who could ask a woman he just met about the sanitary protection she used would have no trouble making some kind of move, but apparently, this was Sid. There were only looks, held studiously, for longer than necessary. Occasionally, there was a peculiar compliment, flirtatious only in an odd way.

Once in the building stairwell, they found themselves climbing from the third floor to the fifth floor meeting room. Connie was now comfortable and wore jeans and t-shirts to work, like the other creatives.

First, Sid was behind her, and then all at once, he skipped two steps, lunging to get ahead, till he was standing before her, holding the heavy door open that she might walk through it. He cleared his throat, met her eyes, and said, "Would you permit a candid comment?"

She stared at him, bewildered by the quaint phrase.

"Sorry, I had to overtake, but you're too sexy for me to walk behind."

It was a little like a mild reprimand. And with his words hanging in the air like a fresh, misted scent, Sid then ushered her through the hall to their meeting. He pulled out a seat for her, and then with great deliberation, made his way to the other end of the table, sat down and began talking to someone else entirely.

These were the games Sid played, and that was just one of a motley number of things that slowly, strangely yet surely, drew her in.

Decades later, their niece had asked Connie what she was wearing the day she and Sid met. And Connie could not, for the life of her, say. She shrugged.

"These details, they're not really important. They have nothing to do with anything."

Sid happened to overhear their conversation as he walked by them. Although he remembered, he said nothing. Because Connie was right. These things had nothing to do with the way they loved each other all these years and their entire lives.

Of course, it was her own fault. Her mistake. Connie knew that. It had been a foolish, impulsive decision, one she regretted heartily. And yet also, not entirely. That was also her fault. The knowledge was resolute, a very small, very sharp stone at the bottom of the glass of drinking water that was her heart. She hurt Sid. She never wanted to do that, certainly never in that puerile, wicked, clichéd way.

But she also knew herself well. Given the same set of circumstances arising exactly as they had – the work trip out of town, the phone call, the drink and the walk to the hotel, right down to the kiss, it would have happened in just the same way. And that kiss was the point of no return. The kind of kiss that did not signal an end, but was only a promise of more to come, leading to the leaning in, the pressing, the prolonging.

It almost did not matter who it was. The short-lived college fling. The pal that had always only been a friend. The relationship that ended when she quit one job for another. It would have happened. And unfortunately, for the past year, she was susceptible, in too weak a position to resist.

Sid found out, and at first, said nothing. She came home to find him sitting in a dark room, watching one of his favourite movies in which an older, no less dazzling Audrey Hepburn, is asked by a brusquely appealing Albert Finney, "What kind of people can sit there without a word to say to each other?" And she replies, "Married people."

Connie hated this movie, or to be truthful, she hated the way Sid liked this movie. It was something that pre-dated their connection, shown to him by another girlfriend, and so Connie resented it: what it meant, what it stood for. Maybe Sid knew that too.

Connie put down her purse, and knelt before him in his easy chair.

"I love you," she said. "I'm so sorry."

Sid did not speak for a long time, and she felt very much like she was falling, the floor sinking beneath her.

Eyes still fixed on the screen, Sid sighed, and after a long pause, said he loved her, too. But he could not meet her gaze. "I will not hurt you like this again," she promised. "Really."

Still, Sid did not look at her.

"Yes, please don't."

They sat there in silence until the film ended. She resolved never to see it again. But also, she promised herself she would be better for them both. She knew this forgiveness, so readily given, was not easy, rather it came out of a tacit understanding that although in this instance, it was her transgression, it might have just as easily been his. As they held each other with care, Connie prayed they would make it through this, because they did love each other. And staying together, well, that was what they had both signed up for.

Sid and Connie reached the hospital after battling their way through more than an hour of traffic. The contractions were at that point, not at all painful, just disturbingly regular. They became more difficult to tolerate when they finally reached the hospital. Sid sat on the edge of her hospital bed and sighed. He looked dead tired. He had worked all day long and had not even had dinner. When he got to the apartment, she met him at the door with the bag. They had to leave right there and then.

Connie leaned in against him, finding comfort in his nearness, even though she was simultaneously sweating and shivering in the hospital gown she had been wearing for hours and hours. She welcomed his warmth. He woke up from a doze when he felt her. Every now and then in very uneven intervals, she had to breathe hard from the pain that would overtake her entire body, radiating from very low in her abdomen.

Two interns in scrubs walked in. Both were pretty in the way that young women were pretty to look at, even masked. Connie couldn't help but check to see whether her husband thought so, too.

But he looked at the women, and said, "Listen, how long is my wife going to be in this kind of pain." Connie liked that. The way he said, 'my wife' and liked that he said it.

"It's not really pain," Connie murmured, but Sid ignored her. A contraction flashed like lightning, a sharp jolt that made her feel like vomiting. She leaned on him and thought, if only she could just rest awhile, get some kind of break.

One of the interns checked Connie's chart, and said uselessly, "She's still only 6.5cm dilated."

"That chart was filled in more than an hour ago," Sid said, his tone clipped and curt. "I think someone needs to check her again now."

One of them turned to her finally.

"Ma'am, do you want me to call anaesthetics for an epidural?"

Connie and Sid answered at the same time.

"No."

"Yes."

The girls looked at each other, and one said to the other, "You check her." At that point, Connie's doctor came in, and before anyone could say anything, she checked Connie herself.

"So, we're moving along ... up to 7.5cm now. A little slow, but how do you feel?"

Connie heard Sid say, "Doc, look at her...she can't go on for much longer ..." He really loves me, she thought.

And that was the last thing Connie remembered. She had apparently passed out from the pain. In the end, the doctor did an emergency C-section.

And then she remembered opening her eyes and seeing Sid holding their son in his arms, Sid smiling at him the way he smiled at her in the past. Then Sid glanced at her and reached for her hand. Her joy was instant, comforting, and enduring, even in her memory.

Sid seemed fuzzy to Connie. His words. His thoughts. The way he was thinking. If it were possible, Sid seemed even fuzzier than it had been yesterday, or was it the day before? And certainly, he was more difficult now than in the weeks and months prior. It was happening. This thing that she had feared. That she would be in this terrifying position of being in charge, of taking care of him for the rest of their lives.

Sid reached for her hand and looked in her eyes and lingered there. He squeezed it, tight and affectionate and even leaned in for a kiss. All across the many years, Connie had relied upon that, and it was a warming in her heart. Even though the words Sid was saying were almost unintelligible, the gesture sent her heart into a spasm that threatened to shatter it, as though her heart were made of glass.

Sid grunted repeatedly. Or it could have been a word or a series of words. Connie was not sure.

There were a lot of grunts these days, and it didn't help that they were the worst kind of days – sections of time that looked similar because nothing really happened, and yet felt long as they were passing. They went for walks. They watched television. They drank cups of tea and had small, easy, bland meals. They had naps. These days weighed heavy on her. They had a happy hour twice a week – one glass each, wine, sometimes a light beer. Like a little date night. She'd always looked forward to those. Sid was trying to tell her something.

He was asking for a glass of water. Connie sighed.

They lived in a house with stairs. Of late, the stairs were becoming less and less manageable for her. She was sure the pitcher they kept upstairs was empty now. She wished that years ago, she had said yes to Sid when he proposed keeping a fridge in their bedroom. The stairs would present the usual problem; she would have to take them slowly to protect her knee, which was crazy, because all day, she had been up and down them, hadn't she? Or was that the day before? She hadn't thought about her knee in months. Maybe it was because she hadn't felt the pain in a while. And now, all of a sudden, here it was.

She should have stopped running when Sid did, and maybe she wouldn't have these sudden attacks on her knee. And now, she was caring for someone whose knees were fine, functionally, but whose movement was impaired. She had read somewhere a long time ago, that was what a stroke did, impair people. That was the word. Impaired. It made them fuzzy. And so she went down the stairs, taking each step with care, with both feet – first one, then the other, on every level.

She heard music playing – a favourite song, one they both liked, a standard and an oldie even when they were young and loved it. He would take her and spin her around and lead her into a dip. Down Connie went with another two-footed step, her own throat feeling dry now. They were not shy. They always used to dance when a good song played. Friends would say, There's Connie and Sid: they will dance. They always danced. But it had to be the right song. She sat herself down on the stairs all of a sudden to take a breath and rest. She heard the voice of their little boy. He loved to see Mom and Dad dance, too. She missed that. And she missed their little boy. And the noise of people and friends in the house. But right now, she needed to get back to Sid with that glass of water he wanted. And she needed to get new shoes that wouldn't hurt her knees when she ran. She was sure as hell not going to quit running, just because Sid quit. Sid could do as he liked, and so could she.

"Hey … Connie, I said I would get it for you. What are you doing here? I said, stay there and rest. Look, here it is …"

And there was Sid, all of a sudden, sitting by her knee on the step below her. He held out the glass. Connie opened her eyes wide. Confused, she looked around her. This was not their old house.

"Where are the stairs?" she said, thinking what an odd thing this was to say.

"We have less stairs now. Let's drink your water." Sid reached to brush her hair from her face, and then held the glass to her lips for her to sip.

"Five stairs, not fifteen," Connie murmured again with some surprise.

"Yes … because we moved, remember? That was years ago. You chose this place. You had a hard time with the stairs at the old house. Come on, it's late. We should get in bed."

Confused, Connie leaned on him. He stood and pulled her gently up. They headed back to their room which was much nearer than it used to be. She remembered now; how could she forget. And now, they were both warm in bed, and she felt Sid spreading the blanket wide over them both. He was still talking, quiet and comforting.

"… and tomorrow, he's going to bring the grandkids by to see us. You know we like that. So let's get some sleep …"

Connie nodded her head, and felt Sid's kiss on her forehead. She did like that. Sid's hand reached out and she felt him squeeze hers with care, feeling it even with her eyes shut. She struggled to find a word. Love. Connie felt her brain go fuzzy and slow. But the word was clear. After all these years, there was that. Love. And that was the only thing that mattered.

AUTHOR'S NOTE

The seed of this story, the germ of it, anyway came to me a few years ago, but I did not write it because I was engrossed in other work. In fact, I didn't know the ending or even the various things that would happen to these two people. I also didn't know it was a love story, as such. It was only when I started writing it that I realised that no matter what, when two people make the decision to get married – on that day, at that moment, they love each other, genuinely. Why would they get married, if they didn't? And it almost doesn't matter what happens to them in the course of the many years they are together. Of course, they can forget that love. Both people can change and change irrevocably. Many different things can happen to two people over the course of a life, but I had this idea that is somewhat philosophical. And that is, if two people can remember something – feeling a feeling or an emotion – that feeling in the remembering of it, of course, comes back to life and becomes real. Memory is reality. Remembering makes real.

The other thing I thought about was a piece of advice from one of my creative writing professors, Michael Mott. He said that the most powerful writing comes from confronting something that you fear. I have friends and relatives that have been affected by dementia and even Alzheimer's disease, and that remains for me a great and tremendous fear.

This story was the opportunity to come up close and touch that fear. At any rate, writing a love story, especially in this day and age, is a difficult thing. It's all too easy to slip in charted territory and fall into recognised patterns and things people have seen or read about already. The nature of genuine love is that it surprises. I wanted that kind of surprise to be at work in the piece, and be like real life in that way that people can be unexpected. Just when you think you know someone, they surprise you – with any luck, in a good and beautiful way. Every marriage comes to points of reckoning in various ways, and not every couple is able to endure that. But Connie and Sid do.

TAKE BACK TIME

AYSHA BAQIR

★ ★ ★

What was the saying about bad luck bundled in threes?

Shirin stared at the screen. Unbelievable. She'd cancelled her 45th birthday celebrations, braved stock-outs of noodles, chilli sauce, and toilet paper, and survived the restructuring plan at her company. But it wasn't over. Now her boss wanted her to rethink retail.

"I encourage you to lead your team to work closely with Tech Solutions, to plan the future marketing strategy for the business. The meeting with Mr. Tan has been set for 10pm tonight."

Shirin frowned and leaned back on the ergonomic chair in her two-bedroom condo in Marina overlooking the harbour. Her father had warned her not to risk her twenty-year plus corporate career in the US to head the marketing director role at a retail group in Singapore, but last autumn, she was eager for change and Singapore, the heart of culture, cuisine and corporates, held exciting opportunities to explore the Far East. That was before the viral tsunami of Covid-19 had rushed in to still the world.

During the circuit breaker, hours had merged into days and weeks while she led her team to develop a new strategy but now, her boss wanted her to collaborate with a tech company she knew nothing about. Shirin ran her fingers through her shoulder-length hair, stood up and walked to the full-length glass window. *Where was the full autonomy in decision-making that she had been promised?* Her hazel eyes scanned the clear blue skies streaked with wispy clouds and settled on the expanse of the water that shimmered like glass.

She breathed in and exhaled. Her team depended on her.

Six hours later, rain lashed the full-length glass window when Shirin switched on the desk lamp and straightened her dress shirt over her pajama bottoms. She checked her notebook once again and clicked on the link. In seconds, she was in the meeting space. Her smiling yet astute associate, Tina, was there along with Mr. Tan, in a blue shirt and glasses.

"Thank you for joining," began Mr. Tan and then paused. Shirin's smile froze. A *Mr. K Ahmad* was requesting to join the meeting. Her breath stuck in her throat. Her chest jammed. She was seeing things.

She wasn't.

He was in front of her. *Kassim.* The easy smile, the deep brown eyes, and the strong stubborn jawline dominated the screen. For one wild moment, she wanted to get up and run but she jammed, unable to move. Something fiery snapped and unleashed from within her chest like a slingshot to the wet-monsoon morning twenty-five years ago. Rushing from different directions, they had almost collided in front of their discussion room. He'd apologised and opened the door to let her in. Since the other team members had already paired up, they had sat together to discuss the reading for their class. Shirin winced.

"Shirin, are you still with us?" Tina's voice was tinged with concern.

"I'm here." Shirin released her fists.

The screen zoomed into Mr. Tan while he spoke. The retail space had changed and it was going to continue to evolve. It was important to understand customer shopping trends and the sector transformation in the foreseeable future. The new retail was virtual and online. It was essential to keep their online shoppers happy and a cost-effective and efficient way was through customer service and technology. Online retail demanded one-on-one attention and that was what Tech Solutions delivered to the customers. Mr. Tan's face disappeared, to be replaced by the first slide.

Listening to Mr. Tan, Shirin smothered the urge to counter and question. Her team had reached the same conclusions. If Tech Solutions possessed the capacity to deliver the innovative ideas highlighted by Mr. Tan, then it would be a win-win for them to work together.

"And with this slide, I reach the end of the presentation. Questions?" Mr. Tan appeared on the screen again.

Shirin interrupted Tina's enthusiastic "Thank you". Her voice rang crisp and curt. "The ideas were intriguing and worth considering. She looked forward to receiving the detailed proposal to review with her team."

The startled look on Kassim's face filled Shirin with a warm satisfaction but Tina's baffled expression choked her with guilt. Mr. Tan smiled. Kassim didn't. He stared at her. No, he wasn't looking at her – they were in a meeting. He looked straight.

Shirin gripped the pen. She wasn't a twenty-year-old, first-year, MBA student; she was an old corporate shark responsible for the company's survival and her own job. The silent Mr. K Ahmad, like the past, was inconsequential. *Why was her chest tight and her breath shallow?*

Mr. Tan cleared this throat and nodded. He would mail the detailed proposal within the hour and looked forward to hearing from her soon.

Shirin disconnected. Shivering, she pulled up her knees to her chest, wrapped her arms around them and rested her forehead down. For twenty-five years, she navigated her life like a speedboat. She'd run fast, furious and against the waves. But she knew inside and deep within her core, she was damaged and decayed, and now dark waters seeped inside, and pulled her down.

In the hazy halo of the lamplight, she pictured Kassim and herself on that first day. They sat in class together. Over lunch in the bustling cafeteria,, they discovered they had mutual friends.

"How had we not met before?" wondered Kassim.

Shirin murmured something about living in a big city. This wasn't the time to bring up her overprotective father. If she hadn't won a scholarship, she wouldn't be here.

"It was his lucky day," Kassim had said, still looking at her. His eyes caught light and fire when he smiled.

Shirin's heart thudded inside her ribcage. A current flickered between them and crackled above the rattle of plates and glasses. She almost jumped in her chair. A rush of heat flushed her face. In a still moment, she recognised a thrill of something new, an adventure. Disoriented, she'd turned to the girl next to her to answer her question and felt Kassim's eyes on her.

Over two years, Kassim waited by the front steps for her each morning and followed her home in his car to make sure she reached home safely. He was by her side, through months and mounds of papers, presentations, and projects and the stress, laughter and the tears they wrought.

And then one day, in the second year, they had walked out of the Operations Strategy class after submitting a term paper. Dark clouds shrouded the skies, thunder cracked, and sleet pounded the grey paved road. They stood in the brick hallway, mesmerised by the force and magic. Suddenly, Kassim turned to her, held his hand out. "Be mine." She barely heard him above the noise of the wind and rain. Was it a declaration or a question, she wasn't sure anymore. But, without hesitation, she'd gripped his hand, laughed and pulled him into the wild storm on the wet grey road like it was a meadow on a sunny hilltop.

Shirin squeezed her eyes and drew in her breath. Then nothing. No crash landing. No tearful parting. She knew they wanted to be together, but maybe not wanted it bad enough. Her industrialist father complained Kassim wasn't good enough for her. Kassim's conservative mother cribbed Shirin was too 'modern' and not a good cook. When Kassim joined a bank in one city and Shirin took up an offer of a multinational in another city, their friends dubbed them Shirin and Khosrow, the ill-fated Persian lovers, but Shirin and Kassim laughed it off. They weren't doomed, they were free to decide and free to determine their own destiny. Determined and in love, they swore that distance could not separate them. For the first few months, Kassim flew over to be with her every weekend. When Kassim's mother developed pneumonia, Shirin flew over to be with him. Kassim reassured her they would get married, as soon his mother recovered. But his mother never let them be alone. Her presence closed in on them, like a noose. On

Shirin's last visit, Kassim's mother hissed that real women didn't hide behind corporate careers and if Shirin wanted Kassim to be happy, she should leave him. Shirin understood that she was being wrenched and ripped from Kassim, like a seedling from the earth.

Shirin sighed. She had believed in them, but maybe not enough. Maybe like a beginner mountaineer, she craved to climb and capture more magical sunrises or like a first-time deep-sea diver, sought more wondrous sights with every dive. Yet every man she'd met afterwards, including Saad, her fiancé for two years, fell short of the easy humour and the electric intimacy. It was never the same with anyone else. Somewhere in the middle, she and Kassim had "glitched" and messed up until every taut whisper, word, gesture, and action was misunderstood and misconstrued.

A year after graduation, Shirin left the country, knowing he would never leave his mother to marry her. Now Kassim worked in a tech company in the US and she had just left the US. Shirin sighed. Her head was in knots and her body ached like she'd slipped on a rocky cliff. She needed sleep, but it swayed out of her reach.

Ping.

Shakily, Shirin straightened up and glanced at the screen. The report. Good. She needed to focus. Only work would drive the demons away.

Weeks later, Shirin slipped a mask over her face and walked out of the elevator into the condominium lobby. Apart from a few trips to the grocery store and pharmacy, she hadn't been out in months but today, she looked forward to a quick lunch at her favourite deli. It was her first lunch out since Phase Two of the circuit breaker, and she had an hour before the call with Mr. Tan to finalise the contract. She smiled at the security guard desk behind the desk.

"Oh, ma'am," he called out, "good you're here. I was just about to slip this into your mailbox."

Dinner tonight?

8pm

The Gazebo

Kassim

A full moon floated amongst the dark cloudy sky when a numb Shirin watched the numbers rise. The elevator stopped with a jerk and the glass door opened.

"Shirin?" A tall man in white linen shirt and dark blue pants walked forward. She looked into his deep brown eyes with light flecks and shifted her gaze. His hair had strands of grey. She had rushed to her hairdresser that afternoon.

A few minutes later, she sat across from him, wanting to look away. A waitress brought over the water and menus and they lowered their masks.

"It's good to see you," he began. He tapped his fingers on the table. Shirin caught the silver flash on his finger. He was married. Her hands gripped her knees. This wasn't going to work. This was unreal.

Kassim said something about work. He was impressed with her career and had no idea she had moved to Singapore. He'd been here for over ten years now.

Shirin reached for her glass of water and gulped it down. He lived here. Why had she thought he was in the US?

It had been easy to find out where she lived, he continued. He wasn't sure she would pick up his call, so he'd sent a note with his driver. She looked good. He liked her hair. It suited her. He raised his glass and his eyes flashed.

Suddenly, she wasn't hungry. She wanted to get up but she couldn't move. He said something about how she hadn't changed much and the next instant, she was ravenous. It was hot, but she shivered. Her hands trembled and she shoved them under the table.

"Anyways, I wanted you to have these," said Kassim. He pulled out two envelopes from his pocket and slid them across the table.

Shirin shook her head. "What are these?"

Kassim picked up one and read it aloud. A shiver slid up Shirin's spine. "Why are you reading it now?" she whispered.

"There's one more," said Kassim. He picked the other note and read it out also.

Shirin shook her head. Her breath burnt her throat. "I never got this."

Kassim nodded. As he began to speak, his voice cracked. He took a deep breath and started again. "A few years ago, my mother passed away. Before she died, she told me to look in her cupboard drawers. She blamed herself that I never married." He stopped and shook his head. "She thought we wouldn't be happy together."

Shirin stared at him. The first note was from her to him saying she had accepted the job in the US and would be leaving the following week. *She hadn't called to tell him because she couldn't bear to hear his voice, yet she had hoped he would leave his mother and fly over to stop her from leaving.* The second note was from him, telling her that his mother had been wheeled into the operating theatre for surgery and he needed her to be with him. *She had never received the note. She would never have left. But he hadn't received her note either.*

"Wait," she jerked back in her seat, remembering his words. "You never married?" She stared at the silver ring. "But you wear a ring?"

"This?" Kassim held up his hand. "This is the class ring from my specialisation after MBA. No, I never married; came close once, but no. It never felt right."

Shirin voice shook and she lowered her gaze to the notes. "How did your mother get hold of these?"

Kassim shrugged. "I suspect she pocketed the letter you sent me and instructed the driver to hand over any mail I sent out. You didn't pick up my calls or respond to my messages and I didn't know why. Finally, I told the driver to courier this letter. I waited for your call or message, but …"

"I never got it." Sudden tears stung Shirin's eyes.

"Over the years, I even tried to track you down on social media and through mutual friends," said Kassim.

Shirin shook her head. "I shunned all social media and steered away from anyone we both knew, but …" She stopped and then looked up. "If you had received my note, would you," her voice shook, "would you have come to stop me from leaving?"

"You know I would have." Kassim leaned forward then stopped. "When you left, I didn't know what to do. I went a little crazy. We hadn't spoken for a few weeks and when I finally called again, your phone was disconnected. I flew over but by that time, you had left and your parents refused to tell me where you were. How could you have just left?"

Her voice shook. "I'm so sorry, my parents never told me, and your mother made it clear that she would never allow us to marry."

Kassim sighed. "When I found the letters, I was confused and then angry with my mother and it was months before I understood that she was doing what she thought was best for us." He looked up. "Maybe it wasn't meant to be then, but now …"

"Now," whispered Shirin, and then flushed as she caught his eyes.

"It's up to us, isn't it? You've changed, so have I, but there's no going back. The past is like sand; the harder we try to grasp it, the faster it slips out of our hands. What matters is the future and what we make of it. I'm just grateful that I've finally found you, and especially now." Kassim held his hand out across the table. "We can try to figure out if there is a future for us together?"

Shirin, paused, nodded, and slid her hand into his. *It was never too late.*

AUTHOR'S NOTE

Initially, I was nervous about contributing to *A View of Stars*. After my debut novel, *Beyond the Fields*, a story about a Punjabi village girl who embarks on a journey for justice, I penned articles and short stories on social issues such as violence against women and children, child labour, and poverty, and not approached the subject of love and romance. Furthermore, my writer workshops and online writing courses had not taught me to write love stories. But then, it struck me that a meaningful love story is not too different than any other story because it too carries a message. Love, a powerful primal emotion, is a catalyst for oxytocin, a harbinger of peace, harmony and the deepest, most fulfilling sentiment within humans. It provides hope for a better and more loving future. And over time, the more I thought about it, the more excited I became to write a love story about characters that are equal and equitable partners in life.

After writing *Take Back Time*, I feel that writers can harness the power of love in these times to address the rising conflicts and challenges in our world. We need more love stories in the world to inspire us, motivate us to help ourselves and help others, and to come together as one community in this world. I hope my short story, *Take Back Time*, does that in its own little way.

CLOSE TO YOU

DENNIS YEO

★ ★ ★

He gazed out. The row of shophouses and the hawker centre across the road had been there for as long as he could remember but everything else had changed. The people on the street all wore face masks, keeping a metre apart. The Covid-19 pandemic that shut the world down at the start of the year had reduced humanity to a society of uniform expressionless faces. No smiles, no frowns, no moods. Just the varied shades and shapes of masks. You could hardly recognise anyone. The "new norm" then had become the norm now. The *pho* shop he patronised had ceased operations, a casualty of three months of closure; yet another resilient bubble tea shop had sprung up and taken its place. Immediately outside the window he was sitting at was a misplaced stone bench that must have been there since the 1970s, before Holland Village became a cool bohemian haunt where expats and the nouveau riche hung out. It was beginning to drizzle.

Loneliness is such a sad affair
And I can hardly wait to be with you again

She wasn't late. He was early. He always was. He had always been the one waiting. Waiting at the foot of her block to send her to work. Waiting at the end of her day to send her home. Waiting. He didn't mind it. In fact, he quite enjoyed it. There was this sense of anticipation, a hunger that would be satisfied when she eventually appeared. Seeing her lanky form saunter towards him was a secret joy he relished. That excruciating minute knowing she would be within reach and would kiss him as a reward for his patience. Wasn't it Borges who had said, "Being with you and not being with you is the only way I have to measure time"? She gave his time meaning. Time is all we have. All we have is time. He could not think of a better way to spend his time and he coveted it every time, knowing all the time that it would not last.

He knew that cynics would scoff in disbelief. Could anyone feel this way? He felt pity for them. The end of longing, to him, was the end of desire and what was love without desire but a fireplace without a fire. To live intensely and fully was to love passionately and fervently. He was not a romantic, not by a long shot. A sentimentalist, perhaps. In truth, he was more an opportunist, a realist even. It was simple. He had only one life to live, and as he grew older, he was aware that he had to live that one life, without regrets and without compunction. To live that life with someone, for someone, in a lifetime of mutual agreement and exchange, was all that he wished. Lost in his thoughts, he absent-mindedly flipped through the menu of delectable desserts, mounds of ice-cream with whipped cream and a cherry on the top.

So many times when the city seems to be without a friendly face
A lonely place
It's nice to know that you'll be there if I need you
And you'll always smile, it's all worthwhile

"Hey." He looked up. It was her. Her eyes glanced at him above the rim of her mask.

"Hey." He rose, fumbled to welcome her, started forward to give her a hug, remembered that even shaking hands was now discouraged, and watched as she sunk into the cushy armchair across from him. "It's been such a long time since I've been here." She looked around her, shaking off a stray raindrop, then, as if noticing him, settled in. "So, how have you been?" She took off her mask and folded it neatly into her handbag. Unbeknownst to her, it was, to him, as if he had turned a corner in Florence and found himself face to face with the Duomo. That visage always looked fresh to him and he caught himself staring at it as if he was looking at it for the first time. He had never tired of it. She gazed unflinchingly back at him, and he was struck again by her bright full eyes accosting him.

Everything I want the world to be
Is now comin' true especially for me
And the reason is clear, it's because you are here
You're the nearest thing to heaven that I've seen

"Oh, I've been good. When did you arrive, last week?"
She smiled her smile. "You look good. It's good to see you."
Her hair was much longer than the last time he had seen her but was fashioned in the same style, with a fringe that fell across

234 A VIEW OF STARS

her face that always held him enthralled, like a veil that promised both revelation and mystery. She was wearing a khaki t-shirt he had never seen before but he caught a glimpse of her necklace. It was one he had given her, at the end of which was an aquamarine crystal with the insignia of the horoscope sign of Cancer. It looked like the number 69 but tipped horizontally. She was not born under the sign of Cancer. He was.

"Shall we order? You've got to go in about an hour, right?" He waved for a waiter, who attended to them, armed with a mask and face shield. "Could I have a scoop of dark Belgian chocolate with extra almonds, and a skinny flat white for the lady, and I'll have a Summer Berries sundae with an iced mocha? Thanks." The waiter scooted off.

She grinned because he had remembered. He was pleased.

Like an old love song
Gone for much too long
You hear it once again
And it carries you away

"How's things with your family? Is your Mum better?" He could feel her gather up her energy to break through her shell to tell him about her life. He had once cracked that shell. He was once in that shell, with her. They had exchanged texts almost nightly for a few years; watched movies virtually together or wistfully listened to oldies like The Carpenters. Their WhatsApp trail had no end. Admittedly, he was not really listening. Her family was not of any concern to him anymore. He was more intent in watching her, absorbing her essence. The cheeky wrinkle of her nose, the thoughtful tilt of the head, the sideways slant of her shoulders.

He yearned to reach out to transgress the hallowed ground of her cheek. She went on talking animatedly about how her brother had usurped her room since she was gone. He traced the outline of the pink of her lips, silently moving as she spoke, sketching the outline of her jaw and imprinting an image of her mien in his mind. It was funny how he had longed for this moment to have her in front of him and now that it was here, it almost felt normal, like it was just yesterday that they had met for coffee, and time had stood still. Her stories recalled a familiar world inhabited by characters from her circle of friends whose names he had heard of but had rarely met.

Funny, but it seems I always wind up here with you
Nice to know somebody loves me
Funny, but it seems that it's the only thing to do
Run and find the one who loves me (the one who loves me)

The ice-cream was served. As she continued, gesturing more with her left hand as she ate, he could not help but notice her ring. It was a modest band with a sparkling seal encrusted on it. It communicated sufficiency and contentment. Her lilt had gone on to her move to Amsterdam. "Well, when we got there," he could not help but wince at the word "we". It suggested a singular unit that was once her and him, but now meant her and *him*, the Dutch trader she had met on Tinder. He could not imagine her being with someone else, and he felt again that tinge of jealous envy he had felt when she had first told him that she had met someone new. It was not fair that everything he had sown had come to naught and that *he* was now in the position to reap from his harvest. She was the last thing before *he* slept and the first thing when *he* woke. He had discovered that jealousy, coupled with a vivid imagination, was an obsessive fixation that coiled itself around him, tormenting him with dreadful thoughts and horrible imaginings. He thought he had quelled its destructive force with distraction. He had gone to the abyss and back and now found himself once again staring over the edge. He could not go back. There were too many ghosts and voices. He had drifted occasionally into the albums of her Facebook profile, visiting old memories and lost places but the unattainable turning back of time was a grasping at the unreachable. Did all of that happen in some alternative universe? She was now on Instagram. He did not follow her there.

> *Lookin' back on how it was in years gone by*
> *And the good times that I had*
> *Makes today seem rather sad, so much has changed.*

He had not attended her wedding. He did not attend weddings as a rule. He did not see the logic of financially sponsoring the delusional product of romantic comedies or encouraging his friends to embark on such a self-centred enterprise as marriage. He had lost faith in the construct. Schooled by Disney, buying into the myth of spending a monogamous lifetime, never ever being alone again, finding another half to complete you. Love songs. Love stories. All a mirage. There was no 'happily ever after'; only a 'till death do us part'. He had once chuckled at a toddler, restless from the tiresome drone of the sermon at a church wedding, asking, "How long is this going to last?" Relationships should have a five-year lease of unbridled passion and starry-eyed devotion and then renewed on a yearly basis if the spark had not been defused. The adage that familiarity breeds contempt was never truer than in a marriage. He wondered what the years would do to her marriage.

She seemed happy enough for now. Her rose-coloured glasses were newly prescribed. She tried to transport him to the colourful tulip fields, showcase the historical artefacts at the Rijksmuseum and help him experience the cold of autumn and winter but he was unmoved. He did not want to partake of any part of this new life. Home was not where, but who. The miles that separated him from her was now reduced to a metre but still, she was unreachable, as she always was; he here and she there. He felt estranged. He did not know her anymore. She seemed different. How did strangers become friends, then lovers, before going back to being strangers again?

Love, look at the two of us
Strangers in many ways

"I'm sorry I've been so full of myself. How is your work and family?" she asked.

"Same old, same old," he replied. He kept briefly to the facts, knowing that the information was no longer relevant to her. Except for her, nothing had changed in his life. Because of her, everything had. That was the tragedy. His ice-cream was melting into a messy pink puddle. His one hour with her was almost up and the time which they had was all run out. This hour had been borrowed time, a bonus. The sun broke through the clouds as the rain came to a stop. "Let me settle the bill. I'll be back."

Before the risin' sun, we fly
So many roads to choose
We'll start out walkin' and learn to run

At the counter, he turned around and admired her from a distance. He imagined himself a stranger scanning the room and setting his eyes on her and appreciating her poised silhouette enhanced by the backlight, as she checked her texts and surveyed the street. He envied the space beside her. He had been inflicted a mortal wound but he felt no anger or bitterness towards her. To him, she could do no wrong. "Shall we go?" She rose and walked ahead of him to the door. As he pulled the door open, he instinctively put his hand on the small of her back like he used to. She didn't seem to mind. As they stepped out, they donned their masks again.

"Do you remember that stone bench?"

"Of course. That was where we took our first wefie." He led her to the bench and reached for his handphone. They sat down. It was wet from the rain. He reached to remove his mask and felt her hand stop him.

"With our masks," she said. "It's more covert."

He took the picture. No one would ever see it. No one would know if they were smiling under the masks.

There is only one wish on my mind
When this day is through I hope that I will find
That tomorrow will be just the same for you and me
All I need will be mine if you are here

He caught her eye and asked point-blank, "Do you love him?"

Her eyes were cast down. "I don't know. Maybe. One day." She paused. Looked up at him imploringly and asked, "Are you okay?"

"I'm okay if you are okay."

They hugged. Him feeling once again how well they fit together. Her feeling his arms draw her into an embrace that swore always to protect her. For a moment, there was silence and, in that silence, they could hear each other speak.

All my life
I could love only you
All your life
You could love only me

He kissed her forehead through his mask.

"You take care."

"You too."

"Be good."

"Always."

He watched her go, a dark wet patch in the shape of a heart on her butt. He would be happy for her. He would love her still. He stood beside the stone bench. Would she turn around to see him watching her walk away? He knew she would not. She did not. His eyes stayed on her till, like a ghost, she disappeared into the crowd, then he turned and headed home.

AUTHOR'S NOTE

The Covid-19 epidemic has given rise to a deep sense of estrangement and displacement in the world today. The various stages of lockdown and restrictions have resulted in a yearning for human connection that is unprecedented. More importantly, the mandatory safe distancing of physical bodies is an objective correlative of the emotional detachment we feel towards people and the defamiliarisation we feel towards places that we once knew, that, as seen in trending photographs, have been left empty and forlorn. Things appear the same, but everything is different.

This setting is the backdrop for the story, ironically titled *Close to You*, the title of a Carpenters song. Two friend-lovers who were once close, but are now closed to each other; both reaching out to regain a moment in a world that they once knew and inhabited but is now lost. The encounter is bittersweet, both a pleasure and a torment, aptly illustrating a line from Fitzgerald's *Tender is the Night*: "Hard to sit here and be close to you, and not kiss you." It is this tension of reaching out or holding back that characterises the interplay of comfortable stasis and inevitable change in a relationship.

The story is peppered with snippets of lyrics from songs by The Carpenters, like a nostalgic soundtrack that plays as the story develops. The few minutes of the best love songs can revive a love that is lost, but will always remain. We tend to want our relationships to last longer than their expiry date. How do we manage the residue of lingering memory and the fallout of missed opportunity that haunts us after all is said and done? The transient permanence of relationships is not sad. It is just the way it is. The world will go on. Things may be different, but some things will always stay the same.

ART AND ARTIFICE

INEZ TAN

On her 18th birthday, Ixora received a small potted shrub crowned with generous clusters of tiny red star-shaped flowers. The tag on the flowerpot said IXORA, with further information below in small print.

"Hey!" said Ixora, reading the tag. "This is an ixora!"

"Oh, it is?" said her parents, who had not read the tag beyond the price. All they had needed to know was that all their friends were giving flowers to their children these days. Not knowing a rose from a daisy, they had simply chosen the plant that seemed to have the most flowers growing on it.

"You named me after a flower?" asked Ixora.

"We named you after a famous actress," said her mother.

"Maybe the flower was named after her," said her father.

Ixora tried to research the ixora, but grew frustrated when her search mainly returned junk about the actress Ixora Wong, whose minor career had ended years ago in a series of petty scandals. Since climate change wiped out nearly all of the planet's flora and fauna, most ecological knowledge had been archived or lost. The reason why flowers had begun trending recently was because people liked how mysterious they were. Well, Ixora thought, if I want to know more about this flower, I'll just have to study it myself.

She found she could spend hours with her ixora, doing nothing but admire how beautiful it was. She found that she loved her flowers' quiet, how they never tried to sell her something or change the way she felt. Their peaceful stillness was so different from everything else around her, from the constant-chatter smartphone to the smartwalls installed in every building and all the way back to the supposedly IQ-raising apps that had recited complex equations to her in utero. Just by being with flowers, she felt a simple, true connection that she had never known with anything else.

After a few days had passed, her ixora began to wrinkle and wither. At this stage, most people accepted that flowers had a short lifespan, and would soon have to be thrown away. But Ixora felt sad looking at her flower – sad, yet curious. She touched each flower's petals gingerly. They felt papery and dry.

Hmm, she thought, if I get thirsty, maybe flowers do too? She dribbled some water from her cup into the flowerpot.

Her parents, who had entered the room, gasped. "What are you doing?"

"Uh, nothing," said Ixora quickly.

It was too late. Her parents had started a rant. "I can't believe it! How could you do such a thing? Pouring your water into a flowerpot, water is a precious resource you know, you must think it falls from the sky …"

Ixora looked for a place to hide the flowerpot, in the hope that they would leave off nagging her about it. In a flash of inspiration, she placed the ixora on her windowsill and drew the curtains over it.

"The young people these days don't know how to manage what they've been given, so ungrateful ..."

"After all we've done for you, this is how you repay us ..."

"You're going to turn into a wasteful, good-for-nothing person, how can someone like that ever ..."

But their reactions changed completely when she presented her ixora to them a week later.

"What! How did you –"

"Is this – But it's –"

The ixora was twice as large and bedecked with scarlet flowers.

"I gave it a little water every day," said Ixora proudly. "And I think it likes being in the sun."

Her mother, on a roll, just kept exclaiming, "What! How did you – how! What – "

Her father grimly left the room to make a phone call.

When they had composed themselves, her parents announced, "Ixora, we think you could be a florist. We've enrolled you in flower school."

Her parents' friends were impressed, or at least acted like they were. "Your daughter is going to be a florist?" gasped her mother's friends.

"Yes, we always knew she had a special gift," said her mother modestly.

"How exotic! Just like her name!"

"Actually, the ixora is indigenous to Southeast Asia," said Ixora.

"And anyway, using the word 'exotic' is just a way to increase the appeal of something to tourists who don't know any better."

"Who cares?" her father's friends boomed. "Someday, she should work for a good floral consultancy firm, like Blue Orchid. Floral consultancy is a hot industry right now. She could make good money."

"Of course," agreed Ixora, but inwardly she was troubled. How would they ever understand? Whatever floral consultancy was, it didn't sound like it had anything to do with what she loved: the secret inner lives of flowers. Nurturing that, day by day, was its own reward.

Which was why flower school was so wonderful.

The campus was situated on a small part of Pulau Ubin that had been painstakingly re-reclaimed using soil salvaged from rural Thailand. The flower professors were relaxed and dreamy, one with the earth and the weather. Ixora was enthralled. The adults she had known all her life acted like they were worms getting pecked to death by birds. In their view of life, all you could do was writhe furiously until a bird got you anyway or you died of exhaustion. But her flower professors were, well, like flowers – calm and unruffled, perfectly arranged, and always capable of balancing the elements harmoniously within themselves.

At orientation, the flower dean told the story for which she was famous – the time a minister had brought her a wilted, beloved flower and begged for her help. "I see the problem," she said. "I will need seven weeks." "Seven weeks!" the minister had exclaimed. "Can't you do it faster? I'll pay you more." "You can certainly pay me more, but I must have seven weeks," she answered serenely. Seven weeks later, she brought back the flower, fully restored. "As I told the minister, even in Singapore, flowers must be allowed to grow at their own pace," she declared to the incoming class. "They can be supported and nourished, but they cannot be hurried. That is their great lesson for us: they cannot permit themselves to compromise."

Ixora joined the other students in applauding, awed. After the opening address, the students were released to mingle, each carrying a sample from their application portfolio. Ixora held her ixora high, proud that its dark green leaves and strong stem looked healthier and better than all the rest ... until she caught sight of one other specimen. Truly, it was her equal – a lush, dark green shrub bursting with bright flowers. As she drew closer, she smelled a delicate, airy fragrance with a hint of mango. She was smitten.

"How beautiful!" she exclaimed. "The flowers are white and yellow! I've never seen a plant with different coloured flowers before."

The boy who was carrying the shrub said, "The river tarenna's flowers are white when they are young, and gradually turn yellow as they mature. As the dean said, the process cannot be hurried. Your ixora is remarkable. I can tell that you and your flowers really understand one other."

Ixora glowed with the compliment. "My name is Ixora," she said, after they had conversed happily about flowers for some time. "What's yours?"

He blushed furiously, turning awkward. "My name is Greenspan. But I don't like talking about myself. Can we go back to discussing flowers?"

"Okay," said Ixora, and they did, but inwardly, she looked forward to the next time she could get to know this enigmatic boy.

The flower curriculum was diverse and wondrous. In one class, they took turns being buried up to their knees in the soil. "Be deeply rooted," their professor called to them. "But turn your face toward the sun!" In another class, they fashioned wings out of wire frames and mahjong paper, painted them meticulously, strapped them onto their backs, and pretended to be butterflies. "Look around! See the world through thousands of new eyes! What attracts you?"

Ixora instantly locked eyes with Greenspan, who, decked out in bright yellow wings edged with black dots, was deeply investigating a spray of wide scarlet blossoms. She fluttered over.

"I see that you are drawn to the climbing bauhinia," she said pleasantly.

"It is popular with butterflies," he replied cheerfully.

She pressed, "Do you like it as well, Greenspan?"

Again, with the shift to personal matters, Greenspan grimaced. "Of course," he said uncomfortably. "Hey, did you know that local pollinators – "

"Do *you* have a favourite flower, Greenspan?"

He blushed and looked down at the ground. "It would be difficult for me to say if I preferred one flower to the rest," he said finally. "I came to flower school to learn about all flowers. I cannot allow myself to be distracted by falling in love with one." With sudden resolve, he said angrily, "My parents never accepted the way I feel about flowers. They always wanted me to become a financial consultant. They only allowed me to come here because I told them I would get a job in floral consultancy."

They had so much in common! Ixora wanted to ask him more. But suddenly, for reasons that were utterly mysterious to her, she felt like there were butterflies fluttering in her chest, jumbling up her words. She found herself saying, "Floral consultancy is a hot industry right now. You could make good money."

His expression immediately changed to disgust. "A hot industry! So, you're one of those people. You just want to sell nonsense to posers who don't know any better. You would make an excellent floral consultant!"

Ixora was so caught off guard by his response that she reacted without thinking. "I would!" she said shrilly. "In fact, I'm going to work at Blue Orchid! Only the top student each year gets awarded an internship there, and I'll – "

"Class, class!" Their flower professor hovered over them, agitated. "Is this how beautiful butterflies behave?"

Ixora and Greenspan scowled and turned away from each other, flapping their wings extra hard to go faster. Ixora flew over to a group of girls preening by a stand of red powderpuffs.

"I hate Greenspan!" she said passionately. "He's such a poser! And he has such a stupid name!"

"He knows such advanced techniques," one girl sighed. "Yesterday, I watched him tilling soil for four hours. He's so brilliant!"

"He has no taste!" said Ixora. "He told me he doesn't have a favourite flower. How can someone like that ever be a real florist?"

"Excuse me," said a voice. It was Greenspan. Ixora blushed. "I was going to apologise for being surly earlier. I can tolerate a slight to my character. But I cannot forgive an insult to my floristry. Good day, Ixora."

He flounced off, butterfly wings quivering with indignation.

The other girls stared at her. They said, "Aren't you going to say, wait! I didn't mean what I said! Come back!"

"No," sniffed Ixora. She folded her arms and didn't say another word all afternoon. But she hadn't meant what she'd said, and she wished he would come back.

★ ★ ★

Three years later, it was announced that two students had tied for being top of their class: Ixora and Greenspan. Ixora tried to act unconcerned when she heard that they had both had been given internships at Blue Orchid. But when she found out that they had been assigned to different departments, she wasn't sure if she felt relieved or disappointed.

Blue Orchid had built their fortune on their line of specialty blue hybrid orchid arrangements. These days, every five-star hotel, hip restaurant, and posh corporate office had to have a Blue Orchid display. The wealthiest clients were those who were able to pay for a subscription to The New Blue, Blue Orchid's signature flower servicing treatment. Every Sunday night, their displays were collected and sent to Blue Orchid's headquarters, and every Monday morning, the clients returned to find their orchids now blooming in the incredible new shade of blue for the week. On national holidays, the company even released rare, special Shiny Blues that were auctioned off for a few lucky winners to display in their lobbies and on their social media.

Ixora was amazed. She remembered the dean telling them on the first day of flower school that the growth of flowers couldn't be hurried. She thought of Greenspan – loathsome Greenspan – who had been so smug about the way his river tarenna's flowers turned yellow, but only over time. Yet somehow, Blue Orchid had developed hybrid orchids that could change their colour overnight. What floristry was this? She had to know.

After a few months of exceptional work performing classic intern duties like photocopying, buying coffee, and updating their social media channels, Ixora went to her boss to request a transfer to the servicing department. She was thrilled when her boss said yes and gave her a stack of nondisclosure agreements to sign. "Usually, we don't let interns into the department of servicing, but we think you are a rising star," her boss said, with a strange glint in her eyes. "We're glad you've taken such a keen interest in what we do here, Ixora. We think you'll be quite impressed."

That Sunday night, her boss led her down to a classified floor of their headquarters. Ixora could barely contain her excitement as she wondered what she would see – some kind of artificially intelligent nanotech greenhouse? A secret team of highly trained specialists who communicated only through binomial nomenclature and the subtlest of gestures? After months of squeezing herself into pencil skirts and high heels, Ixora couldn't wait to be back in khakis and boots, sinking her hands into fresh soil again.

But the servicing department turned out to be a sunless, sealed room, with a strong odour of varnish and paint.

Her boss flicked on harsh flourescent lights. Machinery whined. A conveyor belt clanked and groaned, laden with Blue Orchid displays. Her boss had to shout to be heard above the noise. "Here at Blue Orchid, we have perfected the art of floristry. We believe that the true florist rises above digging in the dirt to liberate the pure idea of the flower. Behold!"

Robotic nozzles blasted the floral displays with paint – a flat pastel she had just been advertising on their social media as next week's New Blue, which struck her now as specious and soulless. Ixora reached out and touched a finished orchid as it whizzed past her on the conveyor belt. "These are plastic!" she cried. "Don't our clients care that these aren't real?"

"What is 'real'?" her boss asked, making quotation marks in the air with her fingers. "Besides, let me assure you that our customers derive complete satisfaction from getting to show off their latest exclusive Blue Orchids. Ultimately, the flower is nothing; what the flower signifies is all. I don't know what twee twaddle they taught you at flower school, but no one cares about that out here in the real world. So, Ixora – Floral Consultant – what do you think?"

"I think real florists grow real flowers," said Ixora angrily.

"Ha! Don't be so romantic. Just do your job. Make good money. Then you can grow your own little flowers as a hobby, when you retire, or whatever."

As the parade of plastic orchids flashed before her eyes, Ixora thought of her parents, their friends, and the collective weight of all their expectations for her. But most of all, she thought of Greenspan, and how he had lost the respect he had for her when he thought she wanted to become a floral consultant. "I cannot permit myself to compromise," she said. "Thank you for this opportunity, but I resign."

Her boss narrowed her eyes. "Don't forget the contracts you signed. If you try to sell our secrets to a rival competitor, we will destroy you."

"Keep your secrets," said Ixora. "I would never try to profit off your lies."

"Yeah, well, good luck to you trying to earn a living from your dreams," her boss sneered, as Ixora walked out of their corporate headquarters.

It was the middle of the night. The streets were empty. Ixora shivered, wondering if she had made a dreadful mistake.

But then she smiled. I know who I am now, she thought. I am a florist. And florists know that flowers need periods of darkness to bloom.

★ ★ ★

The flower school counsellor had to remind her that technically she wasn't a florist yet. She still needed to complete an internship before she could graduate, but there were no placements left.

"Let me work here," said Ixora, lighting up. "I'll do whatever works need to be done. Weeding, fertilising, repotting – I want to get back to my roots!" She laughed a bit too much at her own pun, but she was so glad to be back that she didn't care.

The counsellor frowned. "It's not as prestigious as floral consultancy. And we can't pay very much."

"This is the right place for me," said Ixora, smiling. "Working at Blue Orchid helped me realise that my real passion is to help other people realise the joy of growing their own flowers."

"It's funny you should say that too. A few months ago … well. I'll let you see for yourself. Go back, far back, by the quarry lake."

Intrigued, Ixora followed the path towards the water. She knew there was a reconditioned quarry lake somewhere behind the school, but she had never had a reason to visit it before. As she walked, she found a new enjoyment in taking time to experience the warmth of the sunlight, the scent of recently watered soil, and the hush of cool running water.

When she smelled the unmistakable fragrance of flowers with a hint of mango, she knew she had found what she had been seeking all along.

She emerged in a ring of carefully pruned shrubs that were overflowing with bright white flowers. The river tarenna were in full bloom, like a view of stars, true to their place and themselves.

"Ixora?"

"Greenspan," she said, turning to see the boy whose face was always in her mind. "What are you doing here? I thought you worked at Blue Orchid."

"I promised my parents I would work at Blue Orchid, but I always planned to quit as soon as I got there. Now I'm free to do what I really want – helping others embrace the wonders of growing flowers."

"That's what I want too," said Ixora, misty-eyed.

Greenspan brightened. "I knew it!" he said. "I knew the moment I heard that you'd left Blue Orchid too. I'm sorry, Ixora. Before that, I thought you only cared about prestige and money. But I was wrong about you."

"I was wrong about you too. You're a true florist. You did all this?"

"Yes. I mean ..." he stammered, becoming even cuter as he blushed. "I'm still working on all of it. It can't ..."

"I understand. It can't be hurried," said Ixora, with a smile.

He smiled back at her then, and she added, "But I can already see that it's going to be beautiful." She had recognised what he was so tenderly cultivating at the very centre of the starry hedges: a perfectly domed ixora, soon to be as red and full as a loving heart.

AUTHOR'S NOTE

There's a Marilyn McEntyre quote I love that I'm sort of referencing after Ixora walks away from floral consultancy: "Sometimes it's good to remember how much germinates in the dark of our lives." Two of my good friends were at a low point in their lives when they took temporary retail jobs at an office supplies store. They weren't where they wanted to be – but that turned out to be where they met each other and fell in love! Taking inspiration from them, I wanted to tell a story that involved doing something you had to do, and ending up somewhere you did not want to go, but finding yourself (and your true love) there in the process. That's also the basic shape of some of my other favourite love stories – Eowyn and Faramir from *The Lord of the Rings*, Buttercup and Wesley from *The Princess Bride*, and of course, Elizabeth and Darcy from *Pride and Prejudice.*

When I was writing this story, I was also playing a lot of Stardew Valley, which was teaching me to let things grow at their own pace. Fruit trees take a full season to mature, and even parsnips (the fastest crop) take four in-game days. Growing up in Singapore, I felt a lot of pressure to excel at an accelerated rate. There was this sense that if we were constantly given more work at a higher (or impossible) level of difficulty, we would develop faster – like my Primary Four friends who were already doing Primary Six exam papers in their tuition classes. The problem with this approach is that there are always hidden costs – exhaustion, discouragement, perfectionism, anxiety, misery. Or you get something that looks impossibly fabulous on the outside, but which turns out to be a counterfeit – even if blue orchids were real, they couldn't possibly be induced to change their colour every single week on demand. Flowers – and the people who care for them – know that true growth can't be hurried. The same goes for emotional growth, or the development of a relationship. But just talking about this stuff gets a little heavy, so I tried to balance things out by making this story especially lighthearted, even a little silly. Because love is a little silly sometimes too.

ABOUT THE EDITORS

 **Anitha Devi Pillai (Ph.D.)** is an applied linguist and teacher educator at the National Institute of Education (NIE), Nanyang Technological University (NTU), Singapore. She is the recipient of three Teaching Awards and a research award. She received the *Excellence in Teaching Commendation 2018* from the NIE, NTU (Singapore), and the *SUSS Teaching Merit Award* in 2013 and 2014 from the Singapore University of Social Sciences. In 2017, she received the *Research Excellence Award from Pravasi Express* for her research on the Singapore Malayalee community.

Apart from her academic publications, Anitha has authored six books, including *From Kerala to Singapore: Voices from the Singapore Malayalee Community (2017), From Estate to Embassy: Memories of an Ambassador* (2019) and *The Story of Onam* (2020). She has also recently translated a Tamil novel titled *Sembawang: A Novel* (2020) to English. She is currently writing a collection of short stories about the Malayalee community in Singapore and editing a short story compilation for young adults.

 **Felix Cheong** is the author of eighteen books across different genres, including poetry, short stories, flash fiction and children's picture books. His works have been widely anthologised and nominated for the prestigious Frank O'Connor Award and the Singapore Literature Prize. More recently, his libretto for opera, *At One Time*, was one of three finalists in the New Opera Singapore Open Call for Composition competition. His latest books of poetry, *Oddballs, Screwballs and Other Eccentrics*, and *In the Year of the Virus*, were published in September.

Conferred the Young Artist Award in 2000 by the National Arts Council, Felix has been invited to writers festivals all over the world, such as Edinburgh, Austin, Sydney, Christchurch and Hong Kong. He holds a Masters in Creative Writing and is an associate lecturer with Murdoch University, University of Newcastle, Curtin University and the National University of Singapore.

ABOUT THE WRITERS

 **Joyce Teo** is currently the Vice Dean (Arts Management) at the Nanyang Academy of Fine Arts. She is also an Ethnomusicologist, specialising in gamelan music and enjoys baking to de-stress.

 **Yeoh Jo-Ann** grew up in Malaysia and lives in Singapore. As a teenager, she dreamt of being a cat or a rock star, but instead spent most of her adult life working in publishing, somehow ending up as features editor of a women's magazine before giving it up for a career in digital marketing. She drinks far too much coffee, doesn't eat vegetables, and exercises too infrequently. Her first novel, *Impractical Uses of Cake*, won the Epigram Books Fiction Prize 2018, and her short stories have been included in anthologies such as *Best Singaporean Short Stories: Volume Three*. Jo-Ann is currently working on her second novel and looks forward to completing it before she tears all of her hair out.

 **Meira Chand** was born and educated in London, and is of Swiss-Indian parentage. She studied art at St Martin's School of Art & Design and has a PhD in Creative Writing from the University of Western Australia. She relocated to Singapore in 1997. Her multicultural heritage and the confluence of different

cultures in her life is reflected in her novels, which explore issues of identity, belonging and cultural dislocation. Her novels include *A Far Horizon* (2001) and *A Different Sky* (2010), which follows the lives of three families through the thirty tumultuous years leading up to independence. The novel was on Oprah Winfrey's recommended reading list and "Book of the Month" in Waterstones. It was also longlisted for the International IMPAC Dublin Literary Award in 2012. Her latest novel, *Sacred Waters* (2017), moves between two timelines, and is a compelling exploration of two women's struggle to assert themselves in male-dominated societies.

Robert Yeo is 80 in 2020. He published his first book of poems in 1971. He went on to write other books, stage plays, chair drama committees, edit plays and short stories, write essays on Singaporean theatre and literature and a memoir and librettos for opera. It is a long writing life which he combined with teaching in institutions like the National Institute of Education and the Singapore Management University. His latest books include his 2012 collected poems, *The Best of Robert Yeo,* and the 2016 play, *The Eye of History*. He won the Southeast Asia Write Award in 2011. Volume 2 of his *Memoirs Routes* is scheduled. Photo credit: Laura Schuster

Linda Collins, a New Zealander based in Singapore, is the author of the memoir *Loss Adjustment* and a forthcoming poetry collection, *Sign Language for the Death of Reason*. *Loss Adjustment* was a *Straits Times* top 10 book of 2019, and Book of the Year at New York-based *Singapore Unbound*. Linda has an MA in Creative Writing, and was shortlisted for the Hachette Australia

Trans-Tasman mentorship. Her work has appeared in *QLRS, Cordite, The Oyster Bay Review, Literary Mama, Swamp, Turbine, The Fib Review* and *Flash Frontier*, among others; and she received an Honorable Mention in a *Glimmer Train* Very Short Story Contest. Photo credit: Malcolm McLeod

Nuraliah Norasid is a writer and educator. She graduated with a PhD in English Literature and Creative Writing from Nanyang Technological University. Her writing has been published in a number of journals and anthologies such as *Quarterly Literary Review Singapore (QLRS), Moving Worlds: A Journal of Transcultural Writing, Perempuan: Muslim Women in Singapore Speak Out,* and *Best New Singaporean Short Stories Volume 1.* Her debut novel, *The Gatekeeper,* won the Epigram Books Fiction Prize in 2016.

Rachel Tey is the author of the middle-grade fantasy adventure series, *Tea in Pajamas* and *Tea in Pajamas: Beyond Belzerac.* Outside her day job as a content and communications specialist at a local university, she enjoys escaping into literature (reading or writing), playing the piano and losing herself in Pinterest. She lives in Singapore with her husband, who illustrated her books, and two children. www.racheltey.com

Elaine Chiew is a Singapore-based writer and visual arts researcher. She is the author of *The Heartsick Diaspora* (Myriad Editions 2020, PRHSEA 2019), and compiler and editor of *Cooked Up: Food Fiction From Around the World* (New Internationalist,

2015). Twice winner of the Bridport Short Story Competition, she has published numerous stories in anthologies in the UK, US and Singapore. Originally from Malaysia, she graduated from Stanford Law School and worked as a corporate securities lawyer in New York, London and Hong Kong. She also received an MA in Asian Art History from Goldsmiths, University of London, in 2017.

Nicholas Yong is the author of *Land of the Meat Munchers*, a zombie novella set in Singapore, and *Track Faults and Other Glitches*, a collection of speculative fiction short stories. In 2017, *Track Faults* was shortlisted for Best Fiction Title at the Singapore Book Awards. In his day job, Nicholas covers the general beat as a world-weary journalist at Yahoo News Singapore. In between, he spends far too much time 'nerding' out on books, movies and comics, and preparing for the impending zombie apocalypse. Photo credit: Joseph Nair

Jean Tay holds a double-degree in Creative Writing and Economics from Brown University, USA. She has written over twenty plays and musicals, which have been performed worldwide. She has been nominated four times for Best Original Script for the Life! Theatre Awards, and won for *Everything but the Brain* in 2006. Jean was attached to Singapore Repertory Theatre (SRT) as resident playwright from 2006-2009, and helmed SRT's Young Company Writing Programme from 2012-2016. Her plays *Everything but the Brain* and *Boom* have been used as 'O' and 'N' Level literature texts. Jean is the founding Artistic Director of Saga Seed Theatre, a platform to bring Singapore stories to the stage.

Vicky Chong graduated with an MA in Creative Writing from LASALLE College of the Arts in 2018. Her works have been published in *Readers' Digest*, *The Graduate, Business Mirror* in the Philippines and *Singapore Marketer*, among others. In 2017, her short story, "Chun Kia", was one of 10 pieces selected for the 2017 George Town Literary Festival Fringe publication, *The Zine*. Another short story, "The Uber Driver", won third prize in the 2018 Nick Joaquin Literary Awards Asia-Pacific.

Noelle Q. de Jesus is the author of two short story collections, *Cursed and Other Stories* and *Blood Collected Stories*, which has a French translation, *Passeport*. Noelle has an MFA in Fiction from Bowling Green State University in Ohio, and has won recognition for her short stories. Her work has been anthologised and published in *Puerto del Sol, Mud Season Review, Witness,* and *New Limestone Review*, among others. She wrote the chicklit novel, *Mrs MisMarriage,* under the name Noelle Chua. She lives in Singapore with her husband, with whom she has two adult children, and she is currently trying to finish a novel.

Aysha Baqir grew up in Pakistan. Her time in Mount Holyoke College sparked a passion for economic development. In 1998, she founded a pioneering not-for-profit economic development organisation, Kaarvan Crafts Foundation, with a mission to alleviate poverty by providing business and marketing training to girls and women in low-income communities. Her novel, *Beyond the Fields,* was launched at the Lahore and Karachi

Literary Festivals and was featured in the 2019 Singapore Writers Festival. Her interviews, book reviews, articles and short stories have appeared in *Ex-pat Living, The Herald, Mount Holyoke Alumnae Quarterly, Kitaab, The Tempest*, and Singapore Writer's Group Forum, Borderless, and Countercurrents. She is an Ashoka Fellow. www.ayshabaqir.com

Dennis Yeo began his career as an author with a composition published in the school magazine when he was in Secondary Two. Today, he unleashes his literary energies by assailing his unsuspecting Facebook friends with a continuous barrage of pretentious haikus. An educator by trade, he is living proof that appreciating Literature, teaching Literature and producing Literature are mutually exclusive endeavours. His dabbling in creative writing has resulted in the publication of four poems thus far. This is his virgin foray into prose. The world waits with bated breath for his yet unwritten dramatic work.

Inez Tan is the author of *This Is Where I Won't Be Alone: Stories*, which was a national bestseller. A recent Kundiman fellow, she has won the Academy of American Poets Prize, and her writing has been featured in *The Rumpus, Rattle, The Adroit Journal, Hyphen*, and *Quarterly Literary Review Singapore*. She holds an MFA in Fiction from the University of Michigan and an MFA in Poetry at the University of California, Irvine, where she teaches creative writing. www.ineztan.com